Katherine Carlson

CASUALTIES

Katherine Carlson

CASUALTIES

with photographs by Candace Carlson

Minnesota Voices Project #9

New Rivers Press 1982

Library of Congress Catalog Card Number: 82-61651
ISBN 0-89823-041-1

Typesetting: Peregrine Cold Type
Book design: C.W. Truesdale
Key-lining: Daren Sinsheimer
Editor for this volume: Roger K. Blakely
Rear cover photograph by Joan Halgren

We wish to thank the editors of the following publications for permission to reprint these stories:

NORTH COUNTRY ANVIL for "Doing the Ark Solo,"
FALL OUT for "Defense of the Night Technician,"
TOUCHSTONE for "Confessional."

New Rivers Press, Inc. wishes to thank the following foundations and agencies for their generous support of THE MINNESOTA VOICES PROJECT:

The Jerome Foundation, The Metropolitan Regional Arts Council, The Northwest Area Foundation, and The United Arts Fund.

CASUALTIES has been manufactured in the United States of America for New Rivers Press, Inc. (C.W. Truesdale, editor/publisher), 1602 Selby Ave., St. Paul, MN 55104 in a first edition of 1000 copies.

For my brother Steven James

CASUALTIES

CASUALTIES

PHILLIPS
VODKA

Tornado Watch in Yellow Medicine

SHE HAD TAKEN THREE BATHS A DAY since she was eighteen, for exactly the psychological reasons a woman takes three baths a day. Now she was twenty-nine, driving down Yellow Medicine County 12 in a 1968 pickup truck, waiting for a tornado to apprehend her before she crossed the state line.

The radio was more static than human voice, and between the crackles the announcer warned: ". . . seventy mile an hour winds . . .", ". . . touchdowns in Yellow Medicine . . .", ". . . go down your basement . . . flashlight . . . keep your children inside . . ."

Edwina could not see the outline of the car in front of her on the road, the car she was pacing herself by. The tail lights were the only things in the wide, whirling grey world that weren't running away too fast. Edwina was hooked on tail lights, hooked on rain.

She began to lose the radio station. As she began twirling the dial, seeking another, she lost her grip on the steering wheel and began to hydroplane. The wheels turned on nothing. She laughed.

"In other news . . ."

Edwina focused on the station.

"In other news, a citizen of Climax was found shot today in the marsh outside Little Lake Bend. Billy Benton, Jr., linesman for Wolverine Cooperative Electric Company is thought to have been killed . . ."

Static. Edwina tried to focus the dial.

". . . relations have been notified . . ."

"Relations!" Edwina laughed again, purely and hysterically. "What do you know?"

It was known, in Climax, that Billy Benton had lived with Edwina Cawl for two years before they married. Couples in Climax didn't live together, but Edwina insisted on it, she wanted surety, she wanted no more mistakes.

It was also known that Edwina had been married before to some Twin Cities man, because she was still friends with that city man's sister.

To Climax folks this was not normal, seeing a former in-law after the decree went through. Billy Benton hated his in-laws, for example. He'd gotten his divorce from Melanie, a girl of the town, left her with two daughters, coughed up his support payments like a man, and hated Melanie and all her kin with the usual injured passion.

Billy was a regular guy. He started up the Wolverine Club for his working buddies, and worked hard like a man ought to, and never gave his buddies the shaft. Most everyone liked him, and liked Edwina too, after they warmed up to her. Edwina was a little strange, quietly strange, nice but standoffish, the type that read books and liked to talk about them, until Billy would shut her up, and tell her to "go to the library, shee-ut."

She did, but they didn't have a copy of *Main Street*. She did, but when she asked for poetry, they didn't have any.

Climax knew that Edwina was from Mortimer, a larger town in the southern part of the state, and knew she had lived in the city for a while before Billy picked her up in a bar, and asked her on a whim if she'd go with him to Climax. People were surprised when Billy brought her back, but his friends gave him credit for knowing how to pick them. Edwina was a pretty woman, a nice-mannered woman, a clean church-going woman who wasn't afraid of working. She got the best secretarial job Climax had to offer, at a home for retarded folks that was supervised by the state. Nobody wanted to work at the home, watching all of those ugly people slobber, but Edwina didn't seem to mind much. When she was drunk, she told good stories about the retards, but when she sobered up she called them mentally handicapped people and was ashamed of herself for ever doing otherwise.

People also knew that Edwina loved Billy, liked to be around him all the time, got depressed if he was off on a job where he couldn't come back nights, drank too much by herself when Billy was out raising hell with the boys.

Static. ". . . high winds, damage reported in Yellow Medicine . . ."

She treated his little girls good, though; the two kids had begun to call Billy's house "Edwina's" because they got good food there. Edwina had a musical low voice, and never screamed like their mom, and when she got mad at them she went into another room. When Edwina's friends, the counselors and cooks at the home, asked her if she didn't grudge it when her money went to pay alimony to Melanie, she often said: "I don't care about Melanie, but the girls can have everything I've got."

So Climax, after three years of knowing Edwina, knew a lot about the externals of her life. She was a small town girl, and didn't ask too much but to love her man, and work her job, and be left alone. Edwina joined the Literary Guild, and had books sent to her by mail that Climax didn't have. Billy and Edwina fought as much as everyone else, and about the same kinds of things. Money. Ex-husbands and wives. Sex. The usual.

Billy fought with his girlfriend about the same kinds of things.

This girlfriend was a byword in Climax. She was a hanger-on woman, didn't like to work, took a job here and there and everywhere, hoping to get fired, which she always did. Then she'd cry, and her mother and father would scold her, and maybe slap her around, before they took her back. Billy liked to buy her plants, and he liked to buy Edwina plants, too, especially after he'd fought with one or the other. One time he mixed up which plant went to which woman, but it was all right, because he never wrote notes to go along with the gifts.

Billy kept his girlfriend when he was married to Melanie, and when he married Edwina, he didn't see any reason that anything should have to ch;ange. When some women of the town (they all knew) prodded him to defend his infidelity, he would always say: "Edwina's frigid. A man has got to get it where he can get it."

Edwina actually couldn't get satisfied with Billy, because she didn't trust him, but that was known only to her ex-husband's sister, Edwina's friend. Billy wouldn't have known the difference between a frigid woman and a not frigid woman anyway because he never paid much attention to women's pleasure. Edwina knew how to fake pretty well, and because she loved Billy she always faked, even when it made her feel dishonorable. She took a lot of baths. Billy's girlfriend was frigid, but Billy didn't know that either, since she also faked pretty well. Once in a while, Billy would visit his ex-wife Melanie for a night, and Melanie wasn't frigid. She was frustrated, because since Billy divorced her, she wasn't getting enough sex. Melanie felt degraded when she let Billy in bed with her.

Billy thought he was pleasing the whole round world.

Static. ". . . fifty-five mile an hour winds around Climax . . ."

It was three years before Edwina found out that Billy had a girlfriend, and her heart would have broken if hearts really did break. Climax commiserated with Edwina, and told her all the details, where they'd done it, who had seen them, and how it was arranged. Billy kept telling Edwina he loved her: "You're the only one for me, baby, the only one. I love you, I'm sorry, I'll never do it again."

Edwina forgave him as well as she could. Billy sent her another plant, this one a strange and exotic cactus with spikes and a shape like a crown of thorns. Edwina went on with the job at the home, and Billy went on working auctions for the Wolverine's Club, going fishing with the boys, and seeing his girlfriend. One of Billy's daughters got sent to the county juvenile detention center for smoking pot and breaking windows. One of Billy's brothers tried to commit suicide and Billy went to Marshfield to stay with him at a treatment place for a week. Billy started to take psychology classes, to try to figure out why his brother wanted to die. Edwina typed the papers he wrote, and corrected all the grammar. She typed letters to Billy's juvenile delinquent kid, all of which ended: "Your Daddy says he loves you."

Then Edwina got an infection, and the doctor told her it "looked like VD." Edwina quietly told Billy, and Billy accused her of cheating on him. Later, he went and yelled at his girlfriend. It turned out not be be VD, and it all blew over, except that it started Edwina thinking.

"But what would happen if it *was* VD?" said Edwina to the doctor.

"Oh, I dunno. I guess you might get infected, and go sterile."

So the next time Billy went "out of town" on a business trip for the power company, Edwina went to the girlfriend's house late at night, and saw Billy and the girlfriend through the window. She watched them a long time. Then she went home, and began drinking vodka out of a water glass, just like she'd seen Billy's alcoholic mother do on their infrequent visits to see her. Edwina stayed drunk for two days. Then she sat down with Billy and took him by the hand.

"I can't live like this, Billy. I love you. I won't live like this. We have to talk it out, work it out."

"I don't want any talk," Billy blustered.

"*We have to talk.*"

"This is my problem, and I'll solve it my way," said Billy. "You have to give me time to think it all through."

"I'll leave you, Billy. I swear to God, I'll leave you."

"You walk out that door, and you can keep walking."

Static. ". . . tornado watch, a funnel sighted near Climax . . ."

Edwina stayed. Billy continued to see his girlfriend. Climax continued to buzz with gossip about it. Edwina continued to drink vodka out of water glasses, and stopped being so nice about Billy's reputation.

"It's like my mother always says," Edwina would say to the gossips, who were fascinated by her self-control and disappointed by her avoidance of gory detail. "Men are always hurtful. If Billy were a woman, he'd be a whore, but because he's a man, he's just fooling around. Now I know why Melanie threw him out."

She never said these things in front of Billy's children, though. In front of the girls it was: "We're having some troubles right now, but your Daddy is a fine man. I love your Daddy."

Edwina loved Billy. She stayed, but kept getting more and more hurtful. Her ex-sister-in-law came from the city, and Edwina told her the story, the real story, the not-censored-for-the-gossips-of-Climax story, cried until she was sick, and said: "Somedays, I think of how easy it would be to shoot him with one of his guns while he sleeps."

It happened on that day that the counselor from Marshfield was on his area rounds, and the friend took Edwina there, and made her talk to the counselor man. This calmed things down for a while. Edwina felt better about herself when she talked to the counselor. She began telling him about her mother, and her father who wanted her to be a boy, about her sisters who were all supposed to be boys, and got boys' names: Roberta, Willhelmina, Carla, and finally Edwina. One day she spent the whole hour talking about how worried she was because her mother hadn't talked above a whisper for three years. Her mother was 'internal', said Edwina to the counselor man, she wore size 52 dresses, she was walled up inside of her body. Her father drank whiskey out of paper cups, because her mother stopped doing his dishes. Edwina told the counselor about Billy, and how much she loved Billy, and how hard she was going to work to get Billy back.

One day she finally told the counselor that she was frigid with Billy. The counselor said: "Well, it's no wonder then, is it? That Billy would find someone else to cater to that need you don't fulfill? From that perspective, can you blame him? Don't you think your resentments are getting in the way of a reconciliation?"

"I guess," Edwina mumbled. "But what can I do?"

"Start working on your sex life. Put on nice underwear. Try foreplay. Talk to Billy about what pleases you. You have to be assertive, Edwina."

Edwina thought about assertiveness, and trying to talk to Billy about being pleased when they couldn't even carry on a conversation about cooked carrots without fighting. Edwina looked the counselor man right in the eye. She didn't usually look people in the eye.

"Goodbye," said Edwina to the counselor man.

Edwina went home and took a bath. Billy came home, and she looked him right in the eye.

"I want your decision now. I want it. Now."

Billy had a date with the girlfriend, and was late.

"I promise I'll never see her again," he said, shrinking from Edwina's eyes. "I promise."

They ate in silence, and Billy muttered his excuses, and he left, quietly, and Edwina left just as quietly, and followed him to the girlfriend's house, and watched them through the window. She went home, and loaded up a glass of vodka, and then loaded up a shotgun and stuck it under the couch. She fell asleep on the floor. Billy came home late, stepped over her lolling, tragic face, and went to bed.

Edwina heard him get up the next morning, saw him take out his rod and reel, and knew he was going fishing. She staggered out to the truck, and put the loaded shotgun in the rack while he wasn't looking. Then she came to him.

"I want to go," she demanded. "I want to go."

Billy looked at her, saw how ragged she looked, saw how mean her eyes were.

"Yeah, okay."

Static. "... touchdown, a tornado has touched down near Climax ..."

They drove out to Billy's favorite woodland lake. Billy stepped into the water with his fishing pole, and Edwina shot him. He seemed to know that she was going to do it, and curled up in the marsh like a naughty, bloody little boy going to sleep. It was then that it began to rain.

Edwina got into the truck, and began driving down Yellow Medicine County 12. When she heard that a tornado was coming straight at her from South Dakota, she figured she would go to meet it. She found the tail lights of a car, hooked on to them, hoping they would pace her out of life or over the South Dakota border. It didn't really matter which.

Static. ". . . touchdown in Climax . . ."

Edwina didn't know how the tornado had gotten behind her, and began to cry.

". . . three more funnels sighted off Yellow Medicine 12 . . ."

The rain was dying off suddenly, and the sky was yellow over Yellow Medicine, and finally Edwina saw the whole road. Dancing ahead of her were three funnels, like three conical teats of a miraculous yellow cow, hanging and trembling like a curtain in her path. She passed a green road sign that was now the only geometric shape in the universe.

Wall Drug 453 Miles.

The car with the tail lights pulled into a ditch, Edwina laughed, hit the accelerator, no more pacesetter, it was a movie where cars drove through other cars and nobody got hurt. It was a movie with Burt Reynolds, it was happily ever after destruction. The yellow funnels advanced on the truck, the aerial flew off the hood, the radio died, the pressure dropped and rose and dropped.

Trees danced their roots out of the ground, electric lines danced into flower patterns, Edwina saw fairly large animals being flown through the air like rockets. On her right, she watched joyously as a barn exploded, on her left were two cars being picked up and danced by a large funnel child.

She heard a noise over her truck like a freight train, a rumbling shrieking sound. Two funnels did a minuet before her, seemed to cross one another and merge. A huge elm knelt before the truck, Edwina shifted into four wheel drive, plunged into the ditch and out again, saw that one of the funnels was coming towards her on the road. She kept driving. The funnel took a sudden plunge to the side. In wonder, she watched it crouch, touch the ground like a finger, and explode a fence into matchsticks.

The pressure rose and dropped. Edwina's nose bled. The blood was salty and sticky, and she wiped it away. A yellow funnel scooted further to the left. There was only one in front of her now, she'd run the line, she'd escaped the others. The truck moaned. Edwina plunged forward, it was on her, she was laughing and bleeding together, woman and tornado intersected. The wheels of the truck were lifted, and the pressure shot like a knife through her head. She turned the key off in the ignition, and relaxed like a dead cat as the truck was spun up, up, up into the air of Yellow Medicine County, dancing like the trees, like the very air, dancing like the poetry that you couldn't get in Climax.

"Captured," she screamed in ecstasy. "Captured!" Those were Edwina's last words in Yellow Medicine County.

The people of Climax knew that Edwina Cawl killed her husband, and most of them thought he had it coming, except his girlfriend and one of his daughters (the juvenile delinquent daughter thought he had it coming too.) They also knew that Billy's truck had been found with the shotgun that killed him, mashed up into a strange erotic shape by a fallen tree. Nobody ever found Edwina's body, but the most popular explanation was that it was pulverized, "pulverized by those tornados back in '76", was what people used to say. There was a small funeral service held for Billy, and a small memorial service held for Edwina, in which the Reverend decried the destruction of the nuclear family.

What the people of Climax didn't know wouldn't hurt them, and what they didn't know was this: A woman with stringy hair and a blood stained chest walked shoeless over the South Dakota border in the rain, unpulverized by love or pressure changes, a fugitive on reprieve from three tornados. She hitchhiked across the country until she found a small town she liked. She melted into that town, decayed into it, like a tornado disintegrates into anybody's everyday normal air and dust.

An Extremely Short Story about the Black Hills

Notice: YELLOW THUNDER, the Black Hills Survival Support Group is gathering NEEDED winter supplies for their brothers and sisters in the Black Hills. They are in need of Medical Supplies, Warm Clothing, Tents, Building Tools, Non-Perishable foods, canvas and other warm-weather gear, for their December 7th massive airlift to the Indian People now wintered in the Black Hills and at Big Mountain. For complete information on how you can assist this important effort, call . . .

"Uh, Leo?"

"Yeah?"

"Leo . . ." said Virgil, pointing up at the sky with his stained leather choppers. "Look."

Leo tossed his long black braid over his shoulder, and turned his rocky impassive face to the Dakota sky, which had been his roof for the two months past. Out of the darkness came airborne packages, wafted gracefully on tiny white handkerchief parachutes. The bundles caught on branches, landed on stony outcrops, skittered and danced into the back of the parked pickup truck. As the bundles reached the ground, the white parachute blossoms turned bright orange tones from the campfire's glow. Virgil began to scratch his head as Leo picked up an object that had landed at his boots like a petitioner.

"What is it Leo?" asked Virgil. He'd been in the wilderness a long time.

Leo looked around at the thousands of packets hanging like ornaments from every conifer. He looked calmly at the object in his hand.

"It's a can of beans," said Leo. ". . . from God."

"Oh," said Virgil.

They waited for the next thing.

Defense of the Night Technician

YOU HOSPITAL BUREAUCRATS don't have to tell me I'm a punk, because I know it. Your "victim", Richard Sebastian Dalton, is not. When he was feeling particularly snotty, he liked to point out the cultural differences between us, he liked to play on his Latin and Greek pipes. The only cultural difference I can see is that he's dying, and I'm not. Admit that this is what really bothers you. You're ragging on me because you think I'm the one who ought to be dying. I'm not a promising scholar of the classics. I'm not anybody.

You want to know what happened last night, well, this girl is going to tell you. Last night I made Richard a bag of gold. Don't poke around in my words for symbolic shit, I mean what I say. I am, as you know, the night technician in this cancer hospital, and my job is making IV bags and chemotherapy treatments for the patients here. I mix all the drugs, inject them in solution bags, label them, and then the nurses attach them to people. That is what I do.

Last night we got an order for a high dose of Methotrexate, to be administered to Richard Dalton (age nineteen, sex male, audit number 442861-1, yes, I have read the charts.) Since most of you folks are paper shufflers, I'll explain what this means. Methotrexate is a chemotherapy drug that is bright yellow like bee pollen, and it works by getting your cancer cells so confused that they don't know what is coming off. It costs a lot of money, it has a way of toxifying your kidneys, and it works real good on little kids. Dora (the pharmacist I work for) had to explain its mode of action three times before I really understood. That doesn't mean that I'm dumb. Dora told you I'm a stupid bimbo, but I'm not. I'm not "linguistically primitive" like Richard says either. I'm cagey.

Back to this dose. It was the biggest dose Dora had ever seen. She went out to verify it with the doctors. You'd be surprised at how often those white coated jokers blow their math. You ought to investigate *them.* Dora came back shaking her head, clucking about "my boyfriend." She told me that Richard was getting the biggest dose in the history of the cancer hospital, and that I would have to make it up for him. I scrubbed up to my elbows, sat down in my sterile hood armed with needles, syringes, and a stock bottle of Methotrexate, and began to plunge, suck, plunge, suck gold.

Now, I know my job. Dora doesn't like me, but even she admits that I can make a chemo faster than any technician in this joint. When the bag was finished, it was perfect, honey fat, marked with a standard, approved, pharmaceutically elegant label, with my initials up in the corner. She checked it carefully, and sent if off to Richard like a love letter, or a fragmentation bomb. I don't decide which. I just do what I'm told. Dora is the brains of this outfit, I'm just the hands.

I don't know what happened next, but I can guess. The charge nurse told Richard's nurse, who told the station clerk, who told the nursing assistant, who probably told Richard. Grapevine are mostly universal. He knew before the doctor and his parents came in to tell him about it. He accepted the historic news quietly, as always. He'd been getting chemos for a long time. I know, I made every one of them. Rumor has it that he only asked one question.

"Will I have to lose all my hair?" he was reported as saying. "Haven't I lost enough?"

See how rich kids have their priorities screwed? When he was readmitted this time, I tried to talk to him about priorities. Hey, kid, I would say, since you've been here last Stan kicked off, and Mary bit the dust, and crazy Dayton is finally sane in the great beyond. Subtleties like that were lost on him, though. All he wanted to talk about was Euripides and junk like that. So I played whatever you call a female samaritan while he droned on about looseleaf notebook inconsequentialities. (That was a good word, wasn't it? Give me a break.)

You're all trying to make a big deal about our talks together on the roof. Nurses and doctors use the roof, too, it's public and non-sectarian, so why are you on my case? I always eat my dinner on the roof, same time every night, because I can breathe real air up there. Believe me, I could have done without Richard and his attitudes. He kept laughing at my food, my yogurt, my stone ground wheat bread, my fresh vegies. Let him laugh. Additives, preservatives, and carcinogens sure didn't do much for him.

Until I started talking to him up there, he would sit in a hidden corner and languish over his books. He was a real sad sack. Melancholia is a flashy word for what he was trying to project. Nobility. Resignation. Angst. I say it's bull. I told him he could suffer artistically on his own time. He was hurt at first, but got over it when he found out that I tell good dirty jokes.

"What makes a bull sweat?"

"I don't know," he snickered. "What?"

"A tight Jersey."

Yuck, yuck. I'm really a card. Sometimes I don't have any pride. The thing is, I'd want somebody to make me laugh if I were dying, especially if I hadn't gotten used to the idea. So I kept it up, and he kept losing it.

"What do you think I'd look like with a beard?" he wondered one day. "I'm going to grow one when I get better."

"You'd look like a clean suburban kid with a beard. You'd look like an egghead."

"Even my crotch hair is going," he sighed.

"Don't sweat it," I would say. "Cut a hole in a piece of steel wool and wear it in good health. Now, what are you laughing at? Richard, you're losing it."

When he giggled, he looked juvenile normal: Clean, thin, sandy eyed upper middle class nice normal. Keep it in mind when you write your blasted report. Some days I made him normal, because I liked him, and knew he had to pretend. Now, I will give you all the sex talk verbatim.

"Lily," he asked me that day. "Are you a virgin? I mean, you're not that much older than I am."

You people think I'm tactless? Ha! Me, a virgin? Not since Lincoln's dog died. Not since Muscles Mike in the locker room of the Climax Muskrats high school basketball team. Not since that man in the bar, and that man in the bar, and that man in the bar.

"I guess not."

"Did you know that the original Greek meaning of the word virgin is a person who belongs to themself?"

"So who do you belong to, kiddo?"

"Myself," he said wistfully. "Only myself."

You try to call it seduction, I think it's a joke. Seduction is something beautiful people do to other beautiful people in books. Sure the poor kid was horny, but he wasn't pushy about it, and I didn't solicit anything. All nineteen year old boys (even classical scholars) are horny, only most of them don't get cancer before they go out and do something about it. Sex and death are your two big invisible issues. Put on your cancer plated sunglasses and listen to me.

I understand you. You see that woman they are wheeling down the hall right now? She understands you too. She's got cancer like Richard's got, only she's older, maybe my age, maybe twenty-two. That sheet she wears over her head and shoulders? She wears it all the time. Systemic fungus has just about got her. I make her a bag of fungus killer every other day. Both of us are pissing in the wind.

Fish or cut line you tell me, okay. Dora must have seen us in the hall talking, near the end of my shift. Richard just told me that he was going up on the roof to see the sky. He'd been crying. Maybe his body was giving him the news. I said it sounded like a swell idea. He asked me if I'd please come and talk to him after work. I said I'd think about it.

Dora made it sound sleazy, that's her style. She's okay to work with, but she doesn't like me. For one thing, I think my hands are more socially relevant than her brain. For another thing, I work as if my life depended on it (it does) and she works because her husband won't let her quit. Finally, I brought a black man to a pharmacy picnic once. She hasn't treated me the same since. He was a good dancer. He introduced me to okra. She introduced me to the process of mixing high dose Methotrexate. Everybody gives you something you don't want.

I talked to Richard after my shift was over. What I do on my own time is my own business. Try to fire me, and I'll call my union steward. I know my rights. You want me to stay away from the kid? No problem. I know he's gone now. He wheeled himself out of this place this morning, and left your accounting department holding the bag. What did I do to him? Nothing I can't own. You pry for the details, always scientific, always dissecting what can't be broken down.

I went up on the roof, and found Richard flat on his back, on those mats the nurses suntan on during their breaks. He looked older. The wisps of his hospital gown fluttered in the cool night breeze. His eyes had pink rims like giftwrapped telescopes.

"So Richard," I said, and I was very gentle, if you can believe it. "The doctors are looking for you. I think it's time for your Methotrexate."

"Look up." He pointed to the stars. "Orion. Ursa Major. Ursa Minor. Big bears and little bears."

"Richard. You're losing it."

I was talking about his life.

I rocked him and he cried. Then I went home, drank a whole bunch of 100% natural organic alcohol, and cried to myself. Then I come in to see you all lined up like the slabs of Stonehenge to accuse me of something that isn't in my nature. I tell you, there's injustice in it.

So I evilly seduced a boy who (your shrink tells you) has massive insecurities about sex. So Richard told you that I did that. He tells you that I fastened on to him like an evil tarantula, despoiled his innocence, and then laughed at him. He tells you that I threatened to poison his bags if he told anyone about it. He tells you he's afraid of me, and won't come back for his treatments until you get rid of me. He hates me because I told him the only truth I know, and you didn't prepare him to hear it. He hates me because he's losing it, and I'm gaining it back.

Ask his sky full of bears, they were watching it all. I've tried so hard to be respectable here, but it's blown now. Richard didn't spray my insides with gold. He sprayed my reputation with garbage. I forgive him, because he's dying. It is all of you, judging me, calling me a liar because I'm not like you, that I can't forgive. Why are you doing this to me? Wasn't I a pair of good hands? I did your dirty reality job for you. What more do you want from me? Finesse?

Artificial Rain

AFTER THE DINNER HOUR in the Mississippi Courts, the residents came to roost on the front steps like chickens in a baked barnyard. That day, all the inmates were stretched out in varying degrees of exhaustion on the cement, or on the sparse patch of grass bordering each of the fifty apartment units in this low income housing project. The primary occupations: fanning themselves with rolled up newspapers, bitching about the week long marathon of sticky heat, and drinking beer. The primary entertainment: watching Stan the bohunk watering his droopy petunias.

John O'Neil and his wife Celia were similarly engaged, and sat, feeling hot, tired, and depressed, on the steps of 4942. John would occasionally brush his damp fingers through his prematurely grey hair.

"Life is a grab bag," John sighed. "Everything is closing in on me."

"Yes, the air is so thick," Celia said, intentionally misinterpreting him. "It has to get better. Maybe tomorrow. Maybe it'll rain."

Today, John's boss had been selectively nasty to him, giving him degrading and contradictory orders, trying to confuse and belittle him, the "new kid" at the company. The abuse he had to put up with was gut-wrenching. He was still strong enough to floor the old fart, and only two years ago would have done just that. But two years ago he'd had a good job. Between now and then had been months of unemployment. With a wife and kids to support, John O'Neil could not afford pride, and he knew it. Some nights it became terrifying, and he howled against it, this loss of pride. Tonight was such a night.

Some provider I am, he mused. An errand boy for a lot of jerks stupider than I am. I have a nowhere job as a nowhere mail boy, and I'm thirty-five years old. I should have done better with my life. But it's a grab bag, and always was. How could the factory have laid me off, after seven good years?

Then John's ulcer was acting up. He'd begun to accept the pain again, with stoic resignation. Today Celia had caught him vomiting up bile, and she'd broken down and cried because she knew a secret—one that John knew now. She was pregnant again. Calendars and thermometers might be good for other women, but not for Celia. John would once more be a father, and the web would close tighter, giving the idea of flight a terrible appeal. But at least I can touch her now, he thought sadly, because nothing worse can happen to us.

Celia wouldn't have agreed. She tried not to think about what that worst was, because thought gave it the color of reality. Damn that Edna, Celia thought tangentially. Edna had been talking, bragging, to the neighbor women from her front steps the other day, while John had been mowing the tiny patch of O'Neil lawn.

"I get provided better by welfare than I ever did with that no-good Harvey. I let the State take care of my kids."

"Is that the answer for all of us working stiffs, huh?" John had retorted from across the yard. "Maybe we all ought to run off and let our kids go without fathers?"

Had he considered it? Celia didn't know, but instinct told her that it was possible for any man, however strong, to have a breaking point.

Her children stole into her thoughts, not softly. They always seemed to pick the best times to provoke him. Today they had refused to eat their vegetables, and John had exploded. If they were only old enough to understand how their father suffered daily humiliations so that they could eat! But they were too young. Celia leaned against her husband and smiled bitterly at Stan and his weak petunias.

In their small shared bedroom, the O'Neil girls were also rehashing this dinner incident.

"I didn't think she'd find 'em," the five year old with blue eyes protested. "I hid 'em real good."

"It was funny, though," said Lainy, poking her little sister. "Mom picking up your plate, and seeing the whole ring of peas underneath."

"Well, what were you gonna do with all the ones in your pocket, smarty?" Mary answered.

"Throw 'em down the heat grate. Nobody ever knows what goes down there. Why, just the other day mom was worrying about this piece of paper from the 'lectric company, and when she wasn't looking I just threw it right down. Wasn't that a great idea?"

Mary nodded sagaciously, in perfect imitation of her mother. It never ceased to amaze her, all the wonderful ideas her red-haired sister came up with.

"Daddy was sure mad!"

They sat shoulder to shoulder staring out the window at the sun bleeding in the west. Children were playing a weak game of kick-the-can down the block. They could hear the Newharts screaming at each other in 4946, spitting distance from the window. Mr. Stan was watering his petunias.

"Think they're gonna let us out ever?" Mary asked quietly.

"Nope. They're probably gonna feed us through the crack under the door."

"Really?" Mary goggled.

"Yeah. Only peas. For six years, or until we get big."

"Lain-eee!"

Lainy poked her, and then they both laughed, falling back on the bed and tussling like puppies. The sound of their laughter reached their parents, who both smiled against their will.

So sat the royalty of the Court, the O'Neils, the Wilsons and their son with the crooked arm, the Schwartzes swilling beer, Cupie the Court drunk in his Hawaiian print shirt, and a hundred others up and down, waiting for something good to happen, like rain.

Stan still watered his flowers. He was the ugliest man in the Court. He had a huge nose, crooked lips, and a shaved Marine haircut. He also had a wife named Linda Sue whom he adored, and four kids who bit their nails and picked their noses. If there was any standard entertainment in the cramped housing project it was this scarred young joke of a man. In contrast to reasonable people, he was always doing something. He did things like planting petunias in places that couldn't sustain life. Once, he strained his back carrying his wife into the house because she had cried about being fat, and he wanted to prove to her that she wasn't any fatter than when she got married. He packed his entire family into the cab of his pickup truck once a week to get hamburgers at the local greasy spoon, always driving off singing "...I've got a lovely bunch of coconuts..."

Today he was not being particularly entertaining. He watered the flowers as if it were a duty, not a joy. Every once in a while his daughter Julie would run up to him and ask for candy. "Nada," he would say. "Rots your teeth, baby cakes," he would say. "Bite a rock, punkin puss," he would say. On the fourth or fifth round of this pestering he began to look harassed.

"Daddy, *why* can't I have a..."

Stan squirted her with the garden hose.

She squealed in surprise. Another spray of water hit her in the chest, tumbling her down in the grass. She laid there, her soaked tee shirt shaking as she sobbed uncertainly.

"Look what Stan did to Julie, John, did you see...?" Celia began, until she saw her husband holding his hand over his mouth to stifle a laugh.

Two sweaty little boys, walking back from the swings, saw this incident, and jointly decided that an investigation was in order. They closed on Stan, who ignored his soggy child and continued watering his petunias, a little more vigorously than before.

"Mr. Stan," one asked timidly. "What are ya doin'?"

"Working."

"Mr. Stan," the other continued. "Why are you squirtin' Julie for?"

"Cause that's what I do for bratty kids. I'm sick and tired of kids, and this means you."

The two boys looked at each other and shrugged.

"Heat's got him," one stated confidently. "Let's go."

They didn't leave fast enough to escape Stan's spray gun. He shot them both in the back, and shouted at them unintelligibly as they scampered away.

The general consensus with the step sitters and lawn loungers was that Stan the bohunk had had a bad day. But they all knew it was none of their business, so they pretended not to notice. They also knew that Marie Landauer, the Court busyhead, considered everything her business, and so were not surprised to see her charge out of her apartment.

The old woman marched up to Stan. Her wrinkled face was puckered up with self-righteous zeal. She put her hands on her hips and glared up at him. It was only when she opened her mouth that people knew that something was going to happen.

"Stanley, I don't know what's come over you lately."

No answer. The entire neighborhood knew that you called Stan Stanley at your own risk.

"You should be ashamed of yourself! Acting like a spoiled kid. Making your daughter a wet mess. Stanley, you look at me when I'm talking to you!"

Stan turned around to face her, saying in a careful, polite voice that he never used: "Are you through, Marie?"

"No! And another thing..."

Stan pressed the spray attachment, and watered Mrs. Landauer.

"You...!" she gasped. "You...!"

She dashed into her apartment, her wrinkled hands clenched.

Stan was finally cheering up. He smiled a little and hummed the coconut song, a sheepish look on his face. After a few minutes, he put down the hose, and shuffled up his front steps to get the lemonade he knew Linda Sue would have waiting for him.

He was met instead with a bucket of water, gracefully heaved by Marie.

For a moment he stood, dripping, as the cocky old woman stepped out into the yard.

"How'd you like them apples, Stanley?"

Stan roared with laughter, and yelled: "Marie, this is *war*!"

He pounced on the hose, Marie shrieked, and he began chasing her all over the yard.

Several things happened just then. One of the wet boys hit Lee Schwartz in the back with a water balloon. Cupie the drunk, aroused from his usually stupor, had somehow climbed up on his roof with his hose, and began dousing everyone within reach. Lainy O'Neil snuck out of the front door of 4942 and poured a saucepan of water over her father's head.

Escalation was inevitable. There was a rush on garden hoses and buckets, and the whole neighborhood got into a free for all. Husbands doused wives, children zapped parents, and it was neighbor against neighbor. From the O'Neil's unit the water fight spread through the whole project, until fifty apartment units full of crazy people were emptied into the streets, throwing water over anything that moved. From the highway above the valley where the Courts were set, a wild dance of figures, fountains, and rainbows was visible. Hoards of miniature people could be seen chasing one another, hugging one another, drenching one another with artificial rain.

It lasted a short time, as all great battles do. There were some distinguished combatants. The Wilson's crippled son was found to have a mean aim with a water balloon, his good hand being better than anyone expected. Marie got top honors in the bucket brigade. Linda Sue packed a water pistol like Annie Oakley. And John O'Neil collected the entire neighborhood's applause as he climbed up on Cupie's roof, seized his garden hose, and soaked the old soak to the skin.

The excitement lasted some time after the water had run down the gutters. Lee Schwartz howled when he discovered that his wife had poured his quart of beer over someone's head in the thick of things. Some confused person had called the fire department. They arrived in time to help Cupie off the roof because no one would get him a ladder. One eight year old reported to Lainy that his dad was giving his mom artificial respiration, and she was liking it.

The two sodden generals, Stan and Marie, sat arm in arm on the front steps of their apartment building. She was gasping for breath, and Stan was holding his aching ribs.

"Well, Marie," he got out. "That was...was... a good clean fight."

"You...damn betcha," Marie agreed.

"But there's one thing I have to say," he continued.

"I...shouldn't call you...Stanley?"

"Nope. Marie," he choked seriously. "...you're awful cute when you're mad."

Marie wheezed, and fell back on the steps whooping like some strange wrinkled bird.

John O'Neil, after coiling his water hose, walked over to his wife, who still brandished a plant mister. He was streaming wet, glowing with laughter and exertion, and looked like the handsome young man Celia had married years before. He had a dripping giggly Mary tucked under his arm like excess baggage, and Lainy capered around him.

"Look at these!" he called, indicating his daughters. "What a couple of hellers! How are you going to raise them?"

"With help," Celia responded, accepting Mary into her warm wet lap.

John leaned over her and pressed his forehead to hers. She had understood, then, what he'd been thinking about. It was not because of the artificial rain, or because his daughters looked up at him with his own eyes, but because Celia knew him so completely, and understood him so well, that John O'Neil realized that he would never leave.

"Daddy was a hero, mom," shouted Lainy.

"Daddy is a hero every day," Celia smiled.

The O'Neils went inside together, and waited for something else good to happen, something else good like rain.

Stalking the Historical Fragments

IT WAS AN INSURRECTION faintly delineated in history texts, the action in which Pierre Fontaine died. Fontaine was an impassioned leader of the French 'patriotes' in 1837 French Canada. He was one of twenty-six leaders who were imprisoned in that year for agitations against the British government, and it is speculated that he would have been found guilty by the military court that had been set up for the purposes of disposing of such people, and eventually hung or exiled. The reason for his suicide took many people by surprise (it being personal not political) because, as is the case with most heroes, no one knew what forces really drove him.

The suicide took place in his prison cell. It occurred a few hours after he learned of the death of his pregnant wife, and the 'disappearance' of his two sons, who were given (at ages five and seven) as bond servants to English masters. It happened in the following manner: Pierre took up a sharp rock, and smashed it into his wrist until he drew his own blood. With the blood, he wrote a letter declaring the injustice of war, protesting in agonized terms the death of his wife, and affirming his hatred for his captors. He hung himself shortly afterwards, with twisted sheets from his bed. The letter somehow made its way to his French Canadian friends, and from there it took a convoluted course to some distant relations.

These actions, and his more patriotic activities, romanticized him in the minds of many writers of textbooks that treat the minutiae of military history. He is briefly mentioned in some of the more obscure publications of the period. The name of his wife is never recorded. His sons never learned enough to be able to read about Pierre—they became trappers and fur traders.

One of his sons had a son who had a daughter who had a daughter who trapped animals in the woods one day.

Sandy and I went on a trapping expedition at Professor Barnwell's farm. Barny is trying to turn both of us females into mammalogists, and it's a job beyond even his formidable talents. I should have some kind of natural aptitude for trapping—mom tells me that we have fur trappers in our secret family histories. But really, I could care less if I ever learn it. I just want to pass, and I have a hard time being gracious about field work on a Friday night.

We got lost driving out to the farm. Sandy and I plowed through the rain in the huge station wagon that her parents gave her for being a good girl. She chattered all the way about rodents and insectivores. We chanted together the orders of mammals that we had to memorize: Paucituberculata, Marsupicarnivora, Peramelina, Diprotodonta. We missed the turn, and went six extra miles into obscurity. A couple, scuffing in a leisurely way down the dusty back road, gave us a lesson in corrective geography. When we finally got hooked up to the rest of the class, Barny was right in the middle of describing the types of traps generally used by the working animal scientist.

"These..." he lectured. "...are called, well, mole traps. I'll show you how they work. You find the mole run. That's fairly easy to do, because your feet sink when you walk over them. Set your trap, set it firmly in the ground, one of the prongs on either side of the mole run. Twist it like this."

He demonstrated, screwing and locking into place the rather wicked looking metal blades of the trap.

"When your animal blunders into this plate..."

A small stick was inserted into the center of the trap, at the exact spot that a clumsy mole might insert its nose. The trap whistled viciously as three sharp spikes impaled the air. Everyone nodded, impressed.

"Now. I'd like you to set five of these simpler traps. Do a couple of Museum Specials, a couple of Sherman live traps, and at least one Longworth. I want all of you back here in an hour. Set in a line. Mark your line. Don't lose yourselves. Get to it."

Students gathered around the trap boxes. I grabbed a couple of the Museum Specials (a sort of large mousetrap), while Sandy stuck a number of flat folded live traps under her armpit. We set off south by southeast from the clearing.

"How are we supposed to bait these things?" I grumbled. "Shouldn't we have some peanut butter?"

"Nope. Barny told us how to do it yesterday, in lecture."

"I skipped."

"You put a wad of oatmeal in your mouth, and store the wet glop in your cheek until you're ready to use it. Like this."

Sandy proceeded to gum up a fistful of Quaker Oats. To watch this sorority blondie pulling away on her disgusting plug amused me. I shook my head, laughing.

"Forget it, Sandy. There are some things I won't sink to, even to expand the frontiers of modern science."

Sandy giggled, and in the process swallowed her cache, and had to start a new one.

She set off in viewing distance, putting out her trap line in a slow, methodical way that gave away the talent and expertise behind her fluffy blondness. I watched her go crawling and poking around bushes for good sites. I began my own searches. I dug through humus at several likely spots, and placed my traps, one by one, firmly in the damp soil, baiting them with oatmeal and my own saliva. Whenever I set out one of the kill traps, I stopped and thought, about why I was doing it, about which of my animal brothers or sisters would walk into this manmade deathwish.

I would concentrate on the bait plate. My friend Anya, the natural healer, once told me that by thinking very hard, you could put a strong warding off aura on a place. I tried to do this. I beamed death at the Museum Specials. Death. Badness. Stay clear, little sisters and brothers.

As I set my last one in a thick and brushy glen, I sat back on my heels. There was an envelope of overwhelming sadness about this field that I couldn't split open. I'd trapped mice in my kitchen, and got ghoulish delight out of hauling stiff little bodies out of the cupboards. This was different. To me, in the wake of the teaching of Anya, it seemed like sacrilege to kill and imprison these small ones in their own place. I looked at the sky. It was turning a cold purple grey.

Then, I was kneeling in snow. I was somewhere else. I was someone else.

Child, I put my hand on my belly and feel you, prison of my stomach like the prison in which the man is beaten. The sky of white and darkness plunges against my breast, I see the mountain stream when I was a girl, my face, a human face, torn apart in the icy waters.

The partisans have taken your brothers, little one unborn. They will turn them into white men who kill other white men. The French take my sons from me, the English take my husband. Where are the faces of my people? Broken are they with separation.

"You will never be seen by us, never belong to us. The bargain is final. You will never return as a daughter of the tribe. You have made your choosing."

Empty voices. It was not my choosing, child of no one, child of me.

My father took a small price from the man, such a small price for a human face. I have learned from the man about these things, things which have no value and buy lives, weapons and bright cloth, beads of glass and clay.

"If it had needed guns, if it had needed gold, I would have paid them. Your life is my life. Together we are a nation of our own."

Ah, man, I did not believe you then! Or now. It is a knife in my heart. When your smile has touched the white women, I have felt this pain, and have not believed your words. If you spoke truth, you would not have gone to shoot the others with rifles. Ever the ugly face of belonging-to, leading, draws you forward. The prison wall did not make the crack between us, nor does it take my life.

Sky of darkness, waves of snow which break apart the trees, you cannot see them, child, how futilely, how fatally they crack open. Pray with me to the spirit gods, sing with me how we do not wish to die. Make us, spirit, sister mouse, sister deer, so we do not have to die. We will leap the walls. We will crawl through the walls of the stone place and rest in the hands of the man. Then we will be one nation. He promised me, he promised me.

Pain. So quietly the wind howls. Pain. Young one, you come to my death, to your stopped beginning. On my knees now, I chant to the spirits. It is so quiet in the unending noise. Listen to the laughter of the others, laughing in a language that I do not understand. The splitting trees hide them from my eyes. My voice goes higher and higher and louder than the waves of the wind. My body is a crystal splitting open. Young one, leaving my body, I see you a red crystal, sparkling drops of cold fire on your human face. I wonder why I cry for you. Your pain is over now. You die.

Darkness breaking open, spraying like a waterfall of nothing. It was not my choice. Would you pay guns now, man behind stone, will you pay gold? Am I your payment now? Spirits, make me sister mouse, sister deer. Oh, man of mine, is anything worth this dying?

I am a crystal of ice, a column of air is my center. Make me sister mouse, sister deer. I leap from myself, dead child, eager to abandon the crystal with its braids black ropes in the snow. The last wave takes me, breaks my face into uncountable pieces.

Together we are a nation of our own.

"Hey! Uh, listen...hey!"

I was on my heels in the thick grass, and I was staring at the sky. I looked upwards and saw Sandy's simple face, a mosaic of curiosity.

"Is anything wrong?"

"No," I said. "Just some history."

The next morning we went to run our trap lines with the group. The sun was getting high as we explored Barny's farm for victims. Sandy squealed as she held up two live traps with animals inside of them. My live traps were empty, which is not to say that I didn't catch anything.

In the Museum Specials, I had one animal each. In the first, a tiny mouse lay crushed and lifeless, with a broken back. In the other, a very frightened but alive mouse with a pinched and bloody right front fore struggled. I put the living mouse in a box, put the dead one in my pocket, and went back to Barny.

"Deer mice, *Peromyscus musculatus*, both of them. This one is a pregnant female, fairly young." He tossed her body on top of the car. "This poor feller is a good strong male. He's going to have to be squeezed. You have to be as humane as possible when you sacrifice these animals. Come over here, everyone."

The class gathered around.

"There is one right way to sacrifice an animal this small. As you can see, he'd be crippled for life if we let him live. What you do is squeeze them like this to collapse the lung. They die of suffocation in a matter of seconds. Now, who has something different for us to look at?"

I stared at the stacks of dead animals lying on top of the car in various stages of manglement. I pulled my two out of the bunch, and went off to bury them under a tree together. Who knows? Maybe they were mated once.

I'm never going to be a good mammalogist in my whole life, but I might be a natural healer. Anya told me once that I had a feel for it, that I could open up to the idea of time as a generational continuum. She tells me that strong things echo for a long time in the soul, which is also continuous.

Anya is a really weird person. Since I've been hanging around with her, I've developed an imagination.

I don't need an imagination.

The distant relation who ended up with the letter that Pierre Fontaine wrote in blood is named Cordelia Eumaline, and she is seventy-two years old and lives in Dubuque, Iowa, in a senior citizen high rise. She still speaks French, and wears feather boas when her few remaining preserved gentlemen friends take her to VFW dances. Her hair is jet black, her eyes are brown, and her complexion is orange and weather beaten. Crystals hang in all of her windows, and she keeps mice.

When visiting with the daughter of the daughter of the son of the son of Pierre, she was asked if any description of his wife, who died in childbirth outside of the prison wall, existed in family documents. Was it true, this daughter asked, that the wife was an Indian woman?

Such a description did exist, in a letter in the dusty archives of a French Canadian library. It was written by George Roxbury Mason, a young British officer who discovered the bodies of the imprisoned man inside, and his frozen wife and infant on the outside, both on the same night. He saw to their fitting burial. Shortly after this, Mason resigned his commission and returned to England, citing irreconcilable differences with the army. His letter, which was an embarrassment to his family, read in part: "Her body was broken on the wheel of our insane war policy. She was an outcast of three nations, the British, the French, and her tribe. Her hair was frozen like black ropes in the snow. If my duty consists of driving human beings, even savages, to this type of tragic death, then my duty is a dishonor to me."

Cordelia had seen this letter, in her researches.

"An Indian?" she gasped, her orange face going brickish and her wrinkles dividing her skin into territories. "Certainly not! There is no bad blood in our family. His wife was a highly born French lady. She died of a broken heart in the arms of her lady mother."

The daughter of Pierre's line tried to sooth the old woman, but it couldn't be done.

"I defy you to prove differently," she hissed. "I defy you."

The Perfect Response for Every Occasion

"I KEEP HAVING THIS DREAM about my father, and it always turns out the same. We're sitting at the dinner table eating turkey, and my father has just stuck the carving knife right through the gizzard, and he's eating it right off the point of the blade. Then he makes a stab for the heart, skewers it, laughs, and eats it up in one bite. He's wearing his army uniform, everything, all the medals he owns. So my arm gets a mile long, and I hit him from across the table. I hit him hard, his nose bleeds. He just sits for a minute, then he roars up like fire and chases me and I run and he catches me and sits on me and pounds my head on the floor while the blood from his nose drips in my face, suffocating me, I can't breathe. Then I wake up."

A snort of frost came from the nostrils of the other man in the back of the taxi. He wiped his nose irritably with a monogrammed handkerchief, and shifted himself away from his friend.

"So?" he said.

After the Time Clock

SPEED WAS WHAT SHELLY DID BEST—not the drug variety, but the rate-of-movement kind. She worked at her hospital pharmacist's job like a New York subway car ran, spinning headlong around the stations, past the doctors, through the carts blocking the hallways, up the stairs, and down the ramps. Her pauses were jerky. All of her internal organs readjusted for stopped momentum, and she would spill orders out on the counter in the tiny pharmacy, and sort them for importance. She worked best to country western music, and Emmy Lou, the technician, had switched off to the easy listening station behind her back.

"And we can get married..." Emmy Lou sang, along with the Beach Boys. "...and then we'll be happy..."

Shelly broke before the next verse began.

"It's not that I *mind*, exactly, but I wish you would have asked me!"

These words fell over each other, as Shelly's words often did, and Emmy Lou looked up in surprise.

"What's that?"

"The radio."

"Oh. Well. It was Jim Dickey and the Flat City Mountain Cloggers that did me in," said Emmy Lou sheepishly. "Can we compromise? What about jazz?"

Shelly scuttled from profile to profile, writing down the orders, scooping pills into little bags for the people in the beds downstairs. Emmy Lou interpreted this silence (correctly) as rejection of compromise. She turned off the radio. The irritating thing about Emmy Lou was that she would work in absolute silence rather than give in to Shelly, who was her supervisor officially, and tended to pull rank on the technicians on those rare occasions when she was irate about work. Emmy Lou was sensitive about rank.

The quiet worked on Shelly, as Emmy Lou knew it would. Shelly hated silence. There was a five minute vacuum before Shelly broke again.

"I don't suppose Martin called," she said.

"No."

"He was supposed to call."

"He didn't."

Emmy Lou worked with her own kind of speed, that of an ice skater, flat out in the stretches, careful and low around the corners. When working with Shelly, she did everything exactly so. It was Shelly's habit of picking at the chicken details when she was out of sorts.

"I don't suppose you remembered to pull up the extra oral doses?"

"I did," Emmy Lou offered.

"And the IV slips?"

"On evelopes, waiting for your signature, here." Emmy Lou could not resist adding maliciously. "They would have been done an hour ago if you hadn't lost the order."

Shelly sighed, oppressed by circumstancial evidence. As time went on, it seemed as though she lost more and more control of the superficial things, even of common courtesy. It came to her that she was upset, and it came to her that she was being selfish. For a moment, she thought that if Martin called, it would all be better, then it came to her that it wouldn't.

"It's just that it's so frustrating!" Shelly didn't pinpoint the problem too exactly. "I think some days that it would be so much better if I could just get married, have babies, and learn to play bridge."

"Would that make you happy?"

"Yes. That's all I really want."

"I believe you," Emmy Lou said dryly, affronting Shelly further.

At this juncture, Delilah the nurse came in, brushing back her brass curls to re-pin one of her pink and blue barrettes.

"Hello, ladies," said Delilah. "What say to a beer or two after work?"

The three women had preconceptions about each other. Delilah thought Shelly was a cheerleader, a home grown home town girl, while Emmy struck her as overly judgmental. Shelly thought of Delilah as a tart, and of Emmy Lou as hindered by her obviously working-class background. Emmy Lou saw both of them as confused. They still drank together.

"I'd go for it," Emmy said.

"Let's," Shelly sighed.

So Emmy Lou completed her typing and mixing, Shelly wrote her last note in fat hurried characters, and Delilah shot her patients up with their last pain drugs of the shift. They collected their coats, locked up their valuables, and walked out into the clear bell-cold air, Shelly speeding ahead until called back by the others.

They ended up at Mooney's Pub because Shelly wanted to go there, and the others didn't care. They settled themselves in a place away from the Irish music of the string band, and entertained themselves with talking. They ordered beer. After disposing of work gossip, they made their way to the subject of men, that being the preoccupation of their single milieu.

"So when are you and Martin going to quit dicking around and tie the knot?" Delilah asked Shelly.

Shelly compressed her lips, which were thin and V-shaped. The grimace contrasted geometrically with her eyes, which were tiny crescents and looked oddly oriental. She held her peace resentfully.

"I knew a man once who was very indecisive," Emmy Lou intervened. "He was a very nice person, but he couldn't make up his mind to do anything very fast. It was hateful, if you needed a decision made."

Shelly relaxed, Delilah tightened.

"Why hassle decisions?" Delilah said. "You have a steady man, what are you complaining about all the time? Some of us take pot luck."

"I've gone with Martin for seven years," Shelly said softly. "Do you know how old I am? How old he is?"

"It's a long time to wait," Emmy began.

"Get yourself a new man, he'll come around real quick, honey. Em, are you going to drink that stuff or use it for mouthwash?"

Emmy Lou had ordered Guinness and was having a hard time getting it down.

"I don't know if I could," Shelly sighed. "Get a new man, I mean."

"Why not?" Delilah's eyes were always hard to see. They tended to disappear when she squinted. "You'd have no trouble picking them up. You're the all-American girl."

Emmy had to nod argreement.

"But the rules are all gone. Aren't they?"

Shelly made this appeal to Emmy, who was holding up her brown glass and examining Shelly like a bug through amber.

"At my age..." she continued. "...people assume that you've been around, if you're single, you know, made it with everybody, bedhopping and all that. Now people seem to get to know each other by starting out with sex, and working backwards to love, if you get lucky, and find somebody who will work at all, which mostly doesn't happen, at least not from what I see, so how could I fit in with that stuff? I'm not that kind of girl, sleeping around."

Shelly's words were falling over themselves as she got more and more excited. Delilah examined her resentment with hunched shoulders, hurt by the tirade because she was the kind of person Shelly wasn't.

"It all comes from desperation," said Emmy. "We've all got the biological time clock ticking way down inside of us, the mating instinct. We're all supposed to have our first babies when we're under thirty, right? So what if we're late? Aren't we all getting late?"

No, no, the other two protested in unison, it just wasn't that way.

"But it is!" Emmy insisted, a bit drunker now. "We all want to live in Happy Valley, don't we? Aren't we all afraid of the prospect of living it out alone? Aren't we all waiting around for a man, instead of just being ourselves?"

"That's dinosaurthink," said Delilah, outraged at being accused of having mating urges. "You always were a Victorian, Em. Some of us prefer freedom."

"Maybe," Emmy Lou responded, unconvinced. "And maybe we lie a lot."

At this point a man got up from the table next to them, and he was very drunk. He was young, and dark, a wild Irish rose of a man. He shucked the vest he wore over a rugged blue work shirt, stepped out into the aisle, and began to dance. His arms were rigid by his sides, his face was mummified into impassivity. No motion took place between his hips and his head as he lifted his knees to the music. His flying feet made patterns on the rug.

"What is he doing?" Shelly wondered.

"Ceili dancing," said Emmy.

"Why doesn't he smile? Or move his arms?"

"The conventions of the dance say that he isn't supposed to."

The women watched as the man danced and the crowd cheered his expertise. They all saw a different thing. Shelly saw the rigid face and the arms that wouldn't give, saw Martin staying forever intransigent. Delilah saw the hard precise energetic male motions, and passionately wanted to capture them for private use in the home. Emmy Lou saw an admirable Ceili dancer. The music stopped at the man's feet, and he collapsed in his chair, grinning and sweating, and not the same.

"I'd sure like to dance with him," Delilah said, moved.

"You can't," Emmy laughed. "It's something everybody does alone. Partners never touch."

Shelly finally saw the future and broke.

"I can't!" she exclaimed wildly. "I can't stay! I have to hurry!"

They thought she had had one too many, so they took her home to her apartment, where they left her alone. She sped from wall to wall, whispering: "He doesn't love me, he *will* love me, I'll *make* him love me." The next evening she forced her engagement to Martin. The next week the date was set. The next month she was a married woman. The next year, she was pregnant with her first child. The year after that, she turned thirty and broke the tape and won the race.

She never learned the steps of the Ceili dance. Certain kinds of speed were not for her.

Confessional

"BLESS ME, FATHER, for I have sinned, it has been...uh..."

"Two weeks?" Father Frank Casey hinted.

"...two weeks since my last confession. I accuse myself of, well, of lying twice and...hitting my brother and..."

"You're making things up as you go along, aren't you?"

"Yeah," the ten year old girl admitted. "I really just wanted to ask a question."

Darling Debbie Moran, Frank thought wryly. I wonder what burning moral issue she's cooked up this time? He shifted his big body in the confessional, trying to find a more comfortable position for his knees. He could have had a pillow like the pastor, but he still felt that the hard edges were good for him.

"Go ahead, my child."

"It's about novenas, Father. Now Sister Bethilde told me that if I said one every week or so, I could help bust my grandpa out of purgatory. I'm pretty sure he ended up there. He wasn't very nice to my mom, and he had terrible table manners. A person like that would most likely go to purgatory, wouldn't they?"

Oh Lord, Frank prayed.

"Was he a decent person otherwise?"

"Yes, Father. I was sad when he died. Anyway, I came into chapel yesterday, and was praying my novena, when I saw Mrs. Elsmore Dinty praying a novena too. I thought she had a lot of damned gall. She hangs on the communion rail every Sunday, but she goes home and beats up on her kids and kicks cats. Now this is my question: Is a novena from a cat kicker any good in heaven?"

He could imagine the intelligent workings of the girl's face, and he stifled a laugh. Debbie Moran was one of the Mississippi Court kids, a child of poorer parents who lived in the housing projects down on the river bank. Frank spent much of his time in the Courts, ministering to those Catholics that the congregation of Our Lady of Peace found suspect.

It was one of the many reasons that the church council and his pastor wanted him transferred to a different parish. A crucial meeting was taking place tonight, and Frank was getting psyched up for it.

"Any prayers given to God with good intent hold value..." he began, striving for the easy line. His convictions were not behind his answer, as his mind was politically engaged. He sensed the child's confusion between the grates, but that hardly mattered. Debbie was only a little girl.

After her reluctant leavetaking, he heard a few more conventional confessions, full of lies and false piety. The penances were doled out almost mechanically, as Frank anticipated the impending showdown with the council. They were a rigid group, committed to an irrelevant Latin past, even now in 1964 when the world was rising. If they gave their backing to the pastor, the bishop could transfer him elsewhere, a thing the bishop had already done twice. Frank had a reputation as a troublemaker. He wanted to convert to the new English liturgy. His activities in the black community and his involvement in the anti-war movement were too visible. It was his method of handling the children of the church school, however, that had finally caused the outraged demands for his removal. The girls of Our Lady of Peace were going home and talking religion these days, and their parents were up in arms. Daddy, is screwing Uncle Fred on a business deal okay if you say three Our Fathers afterward? Mommy, why does Pastor Munch drive a Cadillac if being poor is noble? Why does God let there be wars, and race riots, and nursing homes? Why, Daddy, why?

Frank regretted none of his handiwork. He assumed that most of the girls were slotted for a domestic life, but he was determined to make them thinking wives and mothers. How else could they teach their men the meaning of sin?

The next penitent entered the confessional.

"Bless me, Father, for I have sinned. It has been one week since my last confession."

Oh, Coll, Frank thought impatiently, couldn't you have waited for another night?

"I accuse myself of many things unsuited to my calling." The voice was harsh, and very deep. "I accuse myself of ambition. I accuse myself of boredom. I accuse myself of wanting more than God has given me."

He saw the flash of her white cowl through the grate. The head was low, but the voice was frustrated and defiant. Sister Colleen was the science teacher, a heavy middle aged nun with a brilliant mind. She balked at teaching dull children day in and day out. She had been sent to Our Lady of Peace to learn humility, just as Frank had. She wasn't learning. Frank sympathized with her, but in some ways disapproved of her vaulting ambition, her nonconformance, her unfeminine need for limelight. These, to his mind, were not hallmarks of a proper Bride of Christ.

"We must all serve God in the ways He prescribes," Frank began.

"Does God strictly limit his daughters to be menials?" she cried out. "Are we never to grapple with the issues of the real world? He gives me my skills, my mind, my talents. Why must I hide them, when I could use them to everyone's greater good?"

"You commit the sin of conceit, my child," Frank said coolly. "Who are you to determine the greatest good?"

He heard a long sigh. Then, to his amazement, the door to the confessional opened, and closed behind her. He heard her stolid stride as she left the church. He was angry. How dare she break with the etiquette? How dare she decide that he had nothing to give? He was still furious as the next confessing began.

"Father, Father, I want to hurt somebody, I want to die."

Carol Hunt, he thought with growing consternation, this really isn't my day.

"What are you doing here, Carol?" he said through the screen, throwing aside the pretense of anonymity. "Why aren't you at home with your children?"

"Talk to me, Father Frank. Things are getting unbearable and John is away. I only need a few minutes. The children are fine, I left them with Mrs. Moran, she's a good woman but she just doesn't understand things like you do..."

"I have a meeting with the council in ten minutes, Carol. I'll call you when I'm done."

"Too late, oh, please, Father..." she pleaded. "If only you knew what I've been thinking..."

"What have you to confess, Carol?"

His impatience was growing. How many false alarms did the woman expect him to respond to? Carol was another Court resident, married to a hard working man, and giving the poor bastard nothing but grief with her whining eccentricity. As far as Frank could see, her life was a piece of cake. Her kids were well behaved, John didn't drink or run around, her parents and siblings smothered her with concern. Frank thought a good swift kick would do her the most good.

"I confess to being unhappy, Father," she wept. "I'm boxed all around, like a body in a coffin. People stare at me on the street, Father, they know how bad I am. The world is such an ugly place to live, and I can't find myself."

Frank checked his watch.

"I know, Carol, but it can wait for another time. I'll call you tonight. Say a penance, and go home now, there's a good girl."

"Please, Father, help me."

"Go home, Carol. Your children need you."

"My children need me," she repeated.

Carol Hunt went home.

Frank, tired and jaded, stepped out of his little booth of sinners. Life was so terribly hard for honest men, he thought. He was not going to let the council defeat him, or turn him from his mission. The stakes were too high. He felt as if the souls of the entire congregation were on his shoulders. He removed his scapula, and walked like a warrior to the council meeting chamber.

He declaimed, he raged, he beat his fist on the table. His will blazed from his eyes, the will of God, the will of justice. The council argued, Pastor Munch undercut him, but in the end Frank Casey brought them all around to his conclusions. The council reluctantly withdrew their petition to the bishop. He was going to stay the assistant pastor of Our Lady of Peace. He had won.

Later, he remembered his promise to Carol. He called her number. The phone rang again and again and again. Frank felt mildly disturbed. He got into his Volkswagon, and drove to the Mississippi Courts.

Father Frank Casey's last mass at Our Lady of Peace was long discussed. That was the year that most of the Court people transferred their children to the public schools, and began to attend services at St. Brigit's church. This movement was led by Mrs. Moran, Debbie's mother, in an attempt (she said) "...to undo the damage that has been done." Mrs. Moran was frowned upon by some segments of the community because she was a working mother, but when she moved she moved decisively, and took people with her.

That Sunday morning was frosty, and Debbie was bundled up in a variety of mismatched clothes. She always got to church early on Sunday because she sang in the choir. Sister Colleen was up in the choir loft when the child arrived, cradling her hymn book, and tuning up a powerful alto.

"Sister, do you know how Father Frank came out?" Debbie asked shyly.

"No. But the Western World isn't going to rise or fall on the outcome, child."

Debbie smiled, bells rung commencement, and the choir began to sing the processional.

It was apparent from the outset that something was wrong with the priest. He bumped into the altar boys, his rich tenor voice choked, and he seemed to be forgetting parts of the liturgy.

"He looks like he's walking under water," Coll said to herself. Sister Mary Magdalen, fingering the organ like a lover, shot a warning glance at her.

Frank Casey walked up to the pulpit. His strong hands gripped the fine wood and he was struggling to speak. Color drained from Coll's face. She knew this battle, had fought it herself. As the priest looked up at the congregation, she put her hands over her eyes, like a woman who had just seen a part of her own soul. His face was a wall of hate.

"Today I am supposed to speak you words of comfort, words of love about God's tender care of humanity. I am suppose to talk of justice, mercy, and all the rest of that crap. After what I've seen in the last few hours, I have only one conviction. You are all guilty. Every one of you is guilty."

The respected members of the council sat in the front pews, the Court people in the back. Debbie bit her lip as she saw the harshness in her neighbors' faces. She saw her mother in the very last row, clenching her fists together. She had been crying. Debbie recalled the bumps and noises of last night's series of dreams, but mother had only said when she awoke in the middle of the night that someone had died. People died in the Courts all the time.

"I'm tired of lashing whited sepulchers. I'm tired of fighting all of your middle class evils. It was your fault it happened, all your fault. Your wrangling and plotting kept me from doing my job."

"Instead of a sermon, I'm going to tell you a story, a very pretty story. A fine dramatic story, the type you people thrive on. You can read it for yourself in the evening paper, for all the good it will do any damned soul."

"Once upon a time there was a woman named Carol. She was one of your Court people, your dirty outcasts, your pariahs. She had a nervous breakdown when she was very young, so her family sent her to a place where she got to weave baskets, and her doctors twisted her into a normal shape. She then married a good Catholic boy who liked the way she was twisted, and had two children in his name. She had a comfortable home. Her husband took good care of her. The world was Carol's playground."

"Her husband wanted me to teach her the Catholic faith, so I saw her on a regular basis. Some days when I came, she didn't get out of bed because she was too tired. Some days she couldn't hold still, and would walk around the room talking endlessly about her miserable life. These were all symptoms, but I couldn't see it. I was too caught up in your dirty politics to see it."

"She contacted me yesterday at confession. She told me she was afraid of herself, afraid of what she might do. I had a meeting with your council, a meeting this congregation set up to defeat me, to deflect me from my work. I told Carol to say a penance and go home. I said I would call her. Oh God! She needed me, and I said no."

Frank Casey was weeping. Tears ran down his seamed face like rivers.

"I called. The phone rang and rang. I went to her house in the Courts. I found her on the sofa, with a bottle of pills in her hand. I found her two children, drowned in the bathtub, dead. I called an ambulance. I screamed at her, why, why, why?"

"She smiled at me, such a loving smile it was, the smile of a saint. She said to me: Father, you told me that my children needed me, and you were right. I saved them, Father, I saved them. Now they will never have to live in this ugly world again."

Frank raised his hands to an empty heaven.

"Explain to me your will, Oh Lord! I cannot understand. Where is your justice now, where is your mercy? Look upon your servant, Lord, your assassin, your bloody instrument. How could You do this to me?"

A woman stood up in the back of the church. Sister Colleen saw that it was Mrs. Moran. Coll looked next to her to find the child, to stop her ears. Debbie was gone.

"Now you're trying to palm it off on God," Mrs. Moran said in her clear, carrying voice. "Or us. Everyone of us is guilty for closing our ears to her, but you are the guiltiest of all. We Court people kept telling her to go back to her doctors, but no, she wanted you to be her counselor. You and your pep talks, you and your lectures! Playing your self satisfied word games, while she got sicker and crazier. You were her direct line to God, weren't you? She's dead! And all you can think about is yourself!"

"It was God's will!" Frank cried.

"It was *your* will!" Mrs. Moran shouted back. "You're the one she asked for help. You're the one who kept telling her to be content with garbage!"

Mrs. Moran left the church then, an assassin of her own kind. Frank stood and listened to her final accusation ring from the beams overhead, garbage, garbage, garbage. He stared through the stained glass windows in the back of the church and saw her running after a tiny twisted figure in the distance. A small drama was played before his eyes. The mother knelt before the daughter, who pushed her away and walked on. Mrs. Moran was left kneeling on the frosted grass. Your children need you.

"I confess!" he howled. "I confess!"

The mother got up and began to run again.

Frank Casey heard nothing but his own words coming back to him. Before the stunned eyes of the congregation, he dropped his robes of office on the altar, and left the church, never to re-enter it in his lifetime.

Rich sounds of music began to pulse through the church, a powerful alto voice rose like incense.

"May the angels take you into paradise. May the martyrs come to welcome you on your way."

Sister Colleen was singing the mass of the dead.

****

"Bless me, Father, for I have sinned. It has been a month since my last confession. I accuse myself of being a bad parent."

"How so, my child?" said the gentle unfamiliar voice within the St. Brigit's confessional booth.

"It's my ten year old daughter. Debbie won't go to church anymore. I've tried everything. I've threatened, and spanked, and screamed. When I take her with me to mass, she won't say the responses, she keeps her hands over her ears. She was there when, when . . ."

"I have heard the tragic story from other sources."

"I was the one who, I got up and . . ."

"I see," the priest sighed.

They meditated together.

"Debbie is a very good child, Father, a thinking child, but she says that she doesn't believe in God anymore. What can I do?"

"Loss of faith is always sudden and painful. Its return is a gradual process. Forcing your daughter to your beliefs is the greatest crime you can commit. Give her time. Set her an example with the good works of your own life. Now, say a novena for all lost souls, and forgive yourself!"

The Fountain

I HELD HER DAUGHTER. I whispered warnings and corruptions to this baby, from behind the face veil I don't wear but carry inside of me. Cowther held the robe up to her face, pressed it into her chest full of milk, and looked at me as she used to before she became a convert to Islam and moved to an Oregon Islamic community.

"I never thank my husband enough," she said. "He bartered for these gowns. He said 'This is what rich women wear.' "

"They're beautiful robes," I said.

And they were beautiful, in a way that I'm not used to. The one she held was a floor length garb, straight and statuesque, without any bindings or constrictions that would outline Cowther's body and make her shape accessible to men. It was forest green, trimmed with a lively yet circumspect coil of yellow braid. I wondered if, one day, the baby would reach for the tassle on the hood, thinking it was a wandering piece of the sun, and pull it off of Cowther's head as she made prayer. I tapped the baby's diaper to warn her against such a thing. She lifted her baby nightshirt to expose her round tan belly to me, but in a few years she will not be allowed to do this. A tiny robe, a duplicate of Cowther's was spread on the floor ready to conceal her.

"I'll wear this on public days, perhaps at the celebration we hold after the month of Ramadan. But my husband was so disappointed in me. I wish I could be more expressive with him. I should have said more, given him a better appreciation."

"But you never were one to get boiled up about presents, Amelia."

Her eyes were mud pools of devotion.

"He's not responsible for what used to be my American self. He doesn't know what I used to be." She gave me a low and accusing look. "And my name is Cowther, now."

I kept forgetting. She changed her name during the metamorphosis she made from American woman to Muslim wife. I kept forgetting that her marriage was arranged, that she and her husband communicate through broken English and scripture. I reminded the baby that it is I who speak a foreign language here, it is I who 'live as an American.' In the American Islam community that will become this baby's microcosm, living with an American point of view is synonymous with all sorts of degradations.

Cowther lived as an American once, or at least her counterpart Amelia did. I became unhappy and confused, trying to figure out where one began and the other ended, and whether either of them accepted the American me.

"I don't know if I'm a great success at this," said Cowther.

I thought she was talking about being a Muslim, but we couldn't be so explicit as to clarify that. The one question I still can't bring myself to ask is if she regrets becoming an orthodox Muslim, because I'm afraid of what she might say.

She held the robe between us. It was a diaphanous wall.

****

I have a copy of one of the few approved translations of the Koran, which Cowther gave me. The graphics on the front are very pretty, and there is a symbolic modern mosque represented which is surrounded by what look like swatches of Persian rugs. Human beings are not represented in Islamic art, but rugs and gathering places are allowed.

There is a section on women, and I jumped right into it, trying to wriggle my way upstream in this current of ideas, trying to find the hook that Cowther found. The section discussed property disposal, division of women captives, beliefs, transgressions, suitable punishments. It had a sweet and sour flavor, like the soup of cinnamon and tumeric that Cowther cooked me the night before she left Minneapolis.

When it was written, women didn't read. Its teachings were meant to be applied to women, poultices over sore wounds. I open it to find curious rules. Cowther opens it to find pure springing fountains of inspiration. And if there is mud at the bottom of the pool into which the water falls, she must believe that it is her mud and must remain at the bottom of her nature.

My life is not in this book.

****

Cowther was visiting her parents who call themselves Dot and Dub, and they are going to a Twins baseball bame at the Metrodome. The laws of Islam say that Cowther is supposed to honor them, and see their wishes as tantamount to orders. I found them hard to take seriously, especially when Dot lit up a Camel filter and pronounced, in her refined suburbanese grammar, that they would be sitting in the inside press box with what she called the 'mucky-mucks.'

"It's simply plush, Amelia, and they serve liver pate and exotic drinks. The president of so-and-so and such-and-such will be there, and the wives! The clothes! It's all so totally total."

Dot ignored me and talked at Cowther's head, hoping that these urban delights would have some sobering impact on her wayward offspring. Dot wanted Cowther to be jealous, wanted her American spirit to rise up, cast off headscarf and robe, and go scream popcorn scented obscenities all over the Astroturf. She tried to buy Cowther a Cuisinart for a wedding present, and was put out when Cowther preferred plane fare from Oregon to come and see her. Cowther and her mother don't have much in common. God knows.

". . . and couches to sit on, and it's temperature controlled. They'll even have two kinds of olives."

"It'd be nicer if they had some coffee and brownies," said Dub.

I laughed because I thought he meant to prick his wife's pomposity, but he wasn't at all being ironic. Dub likes coffee and brownies My giggle died a natural death, and they all stared at me, looking strangely like a family. Cowther looked like their daughter, then. Context made all the difference.

Dot and Dub asked me for directions to the Metrodome, but I didn't know how to tell them to get there, even though I work only a few blocks away from it and could find it in my sleep. My orientation is not directional, I tried to explain; I never know where I am until I'm close. Dot and Dub were mutual in their unphrased denigration of me, and went away in the car. I retired my face into the baby's hair.

"There was a lot of controversy about it being built, wasn't there?" said Cowther. "What does it look like?"

"Like the pie that four and twenty blackbirds were baked in."

Cowther laughed and laughed, and so did I, and so did the baby, who was so amused that she peed all over my dress. It just exploded out from the rim of her leg all over the rug.

"She's big on secretions," I said.

"Those must be the bum pair of rubber pants," said Cowther.

It was these bits and pieces of Amelia that I came for. Her cynical wit, which she's all but erased, sneaks up under her floor length garb, at times, and bites her in private places. I couldn't tell any good jokes. I live by telling good jokes.

Did you hear the one about the Muslim wife and the American friend, who by touching a baby connected to each other across a widening abyss of religious disagreement?

"Who mows the grass on Walton's mountain?" I asked.

"Who?"

"Lawnboy!"

That was the only one I knew that was clean.

****

I helped Cowther pack. She is leaving tomorrow for home, husband, and her Oregon Islam community. She may live in the Muslim community there for the rest of her life. She may go to the middle east tomorrow, and get blown up in some border war. For complex political reasons, her husband is not safe in his country of origin. During her visit he was "travelling," a euphemism that held a direct meaning for her but was mysterious to me. She was understandably vague about names and dates, since his country spies on him.

She folded the robes that bound her to her husband. I found it sad that her body was now invisible. Cowther has skin the color of amber, and it contrasts oddly with the pinkish sheen of henna in her brown hair. Every now and then she would pop one of her breasts out of her loose garb to feed the baby, who would not sleep, never slept, as long as there were interesting conversations to listen to. I folded up one of Cowther's nightgowns, which was pretty and lacy and sort of American.

"Nice undies," I whistled.

Cowther pressed her lips in. I don't know any other way to describe this. When she does it, she looks like she hasn't got any mouth, and you know it is time to talk about the weather.

"It's getting cloudy," I added, as if clouds and underwear blend into one another on some astral plane.

"I was hoping for a thunderstorm. A real Minnesota one. They don't have them in Oregon. It rains there like a curtain. The clouds don't crack and the wind doesn't blow in that romantic way."

Romance.

"I wanted to tell you about what happened with me and . . .

"Don't," she said, pained. "Keep to the wind."

****

We still can't talk about the affair I had. We don't touch that sort of stuff now, although we used to. My affair was sort of an arranged marriage, in that I didn't love the man, and he didn't love me, but we both wanted somebody to love so bad that we compromised. Compromise, in affairs, is no good. Cowther broke up my affair, in a funny way. When I talked to my boyfriend about her, he had a million scornful and prefab statements prepared. We argued about her. The argument became symbolic of how narrow minded he was, until there was a gap between us that is as large as the one between Cowther and I now. But Cowther and I have love and friendship to rope-ladder our abyss. My boyfriend and I never did. I cried for a whole day when he left me for a woman with bigger tits and a greater ability to compromise. Que sera, sera.

This is the part I can't accept, but perhaps loving the right man is part of my American dream. The odds are against my ever becoming a millionaire, and the odds are against my having both freedom and babies, but I keep muddling along anyway. Islam is more practical. You meet, you compare ideologies, you say yes or no, marry, pollinate, and bear fruit. This looks good to me, now and then, and that is why I object so strenuously to Cowther dipping her long fingers into this particular fountain.

"There are some of the brothers who are not as strict with the laws, but are still good men. You wouldn't want to correspond with them on the subject of marriage?" she asked me.

The baby listened to this one intently. She knew.

Dear Man. Will you admit that you have no right to *let* me do anything? Will you listen to my constant argument with my disembodied God? Will you leave me to pursue the horizon, even on holy days? Will you fast alone?

"No," I said, patting the baby. "That's not for me."

A fist of wind split the draperies, pressed them out straight from the wall, as lightning flickered and thunder rolled at a countable distance. Rain bludgeoned the windows. We ran to close up the house, so that Dot's material possessions would not get rained on. The baby lay on her back and kicked at the ceiling, struggling to see what she could only hear.

"Your thunderstorm," I told Cowther. "It's come."

"I have to pray now."

******

I danced the baby, did the Lindy, framed by the screen door of Dot and Dub's. Cowther dressed again, covered her head in a light colored head scarf and the hood from one of her husband's gifts, a nunlike black robe with a nonreflecting texture. She turned out the lights. She began her prayers, standing, kneeling, whispering, a brave figure of integrity in concealment. The baby didn't know whom to watch. The thunderstorm was special to her, a phenomenon she had never seen. Her mother's prayers she sees five times every day. Both seemed to hold an equal fascination for her. She was distraught, unable to look two ways at once. I sang to her. Shine on, shine on harvest moon.

Cowther pressed her forehead into the rug.

The baby's eyes bounced, like little balls in those old singalongs, the balls that signified which words went with which notes in the music. Shine on, shine on harvest moon. Up in the sky. Natural thunderstorm. Human mother.

"Your choice," I said to the baby.

Cowther once told me that only a very strong discipline could contain all the undisciplines she was. As she got up from the floor and relaxed, the residue of Amelia was gone and she was new. She released a fountain of hair from her scarf and a fountain of peace from another place.

"Oh, I want to go home!" she said.

The baby held out her arms, asking to be fed from the fountain.

Lady of the Dalles

"I DON'T KNOW IF YOU CAN understand, Little Margeen, what it's like to be under watch all the time," said Franny, while she fixed her eyes on a point long, long, down the grey highway. "You're too young to understand, aren't you, Little?"

Margeen twitched in the red bucket seat, scratched a nit bite on her knee, and tried to make believe that she wasn't eight years old and wasn't afraid.

"You ain't gonna do something bad to me, auntie?"

"No. Life will do all the bad you need, more even. Hush for a second, look. Over the hill. See the sun, see how pretty it makes the sky, Little?"

The child saw the sunrise and sunset every day from her upstairs attic bedroom, and the prettiness was nothing new, but she nodded, nervous, upset in her mind about the strangement of Aunt Franny. That was what mother called it, strangement, but when Margeen looked the word up, it wasn't a word and didn't mean anything. Little Margeen really wanted to know about Aunt Franny's going away and coming back, but she figured that the dictionary hadn't made a word for what happened to her yet.

"Where are we going, auntie? You told me it wasn't far two hours back," Margeen cried. "Mom'll worry, you know she'll just be hair on fire."

"Yes." It was a deep pulse of pain, and even Margeen was old enough to feel it hurting in Franny. "You believe what she says about me, Little? You think I'm crazy, too?"

Margeen folded the corner of the paper card in her pocket, the one with all the telephone numbers for "just in case" Aunt Franny "got funny." She began to clean dirt out from under her fingernails with an edge of it. When Franny's gaze left her for the highway, Margeen looked over at her auntie. It was purely a pleasure looking at Franny, and thinking in her heart of dreams that one day she might grow up to look that way, that marble-saint-from-Loyola-Church way, like Franny. Today Franny had her hair all braided up on top of her head like a crown in loose white blond ropes, and she wore a shirt the color of the columbines on the twisted back porch of the farmhouse. Margeen had blond hair, too, but it was short and straight and wheat-colored.

"You got such pretty hair, auntie, I wish mine was like that too."

"What kind of thing does your mother say about me, Little?"

"She says you got a psychosomic problem, and all kind of thing like that," said the child, trapped into the truth. "She says I'm not suppose to go out driving in the car with you, and she's gonna be so mad at me! Auntie, can't we go back? You been acting funny, and the accident happened, and you went away, and I don't know what to do about anything. Not anything!"

"Look. We're heading into the valley."

They plunged down, down into the steady grey rock of the river valley, while the sun slapped paint on the granite surfaces.

"Why, auntie! I remember this place. You took me here, and there was a face of a man on the rocks, wasn't there? And a boat and all?"

Franny relaxed her pale eyebrows then, and reached out tentatively to touch Margeen's knee.

"Tell me more about it, Little. Just to remember me."

"Why, there was a pretty town, I think, and a house with all the old, old dolls, way old, like you and mom used to have. Oh, and auntie, there were horses in the street, right with the cars like they had a right to be there. And we had ice cream. Oh, that was a fine day. And mom and you took a walk in the woods with me, and . . . and . . . oh! Auntie, auntie, there it is! Oh, lookit, something's going on!"

Margeen jumped up and down in her seat, because down in the valley town, there were balloons in the air, and horses drawing old fashioned carriages, and people dressed up in antique clothes. There was a persistent hum of drums from the rear end of the high school band. As Franny and Margeen eased up to a blocked intersection, the band's horn section began to toot out a theme song to some television show. Franny rolled down the window, and called out to a policeman on the corner.

"Hey, mister! What's going on?"

"Town celebration!" he yelled back heartily. "Come on and join up."

Franny urged the car carefully into a side street, and parked. Margeen thought she looked like the old Franny, the funny and joking Franny.

"Take my hand, Little, and we'll go crazy with these folks for an evening. Why, look at those boys, they're going to fall off that truck bed in a minute for laughing!"

Those boys waved coonskin caps at pretty Franny, and she gosh all waved back like she knew them every one. Together they skipped along the sidewalks, and Franny picked up a silver balloon thing that floated behind them all by itself like a spaceship. On the way through the people, they got an ice cream, strawberry home-made kind, and smeared it all over their chins. Margeen dropped her note card of phone numbers in the dirt, and left it there. As the street lights popped on, and the dust settled down, Margeen caught sight of a place she'd been looking for all the trip up and down for hours.

"Auntie, ain't that the place? Oh, please, let's just go in for a minute, I promise I won't pester, I swear."

It was the toy shop. It was an old shop, and carried antique dolls, each with a pale white china face like a full moon. The dolls were dressed in taffeta and satin and lace. Margeen wanted one, but knew now that dolls like those were for wealthy folks, not people of the likes of Margeen.

"You're a big girl now, honey. You can pick one up, if you want to. Just be careful, and don't bump her head against anything, okay?"

"That one," whispered Little, pointing up at a delicate confection on a hook high above the electric trains. "Oh, ain't she pretty? Looks kinds like you, auntie, with her hair and all."

Franny reached upwards, and got the doll off the hook. It was a southern belle in violet and velvet, with a boa around its neck. Margeen rocked it, and in rocking thought of mom, and with mom thought of worries, and with worries thought of Franny, who was just looking like she knew.

"Your mom and I had dolls like that once, Little. Grandma gave them to us, one in red satin for me, and one in green velvet for your mother. You know what grandma said when she gave them? She said: 'Take care of these children I give you, I had 'em when I was a youngun, and they did me good. I used to pretend they was my sisters and when my sisters, who was regular hellers, give me trouble, why, I'd go whump the dolls, but I'd love my sisters in spite of what they done to me. Treat your sisters gentle, and you'll never be lonesome for a friend.' That's what she said."

Margeen knew there was a lesson, but didn't have a sister, so failed to find it.

"Did you treat them good, auntie, I mean the dollies?"

"Nope. I broke mine one time when I got mad at your mom. And you know what?"

"What?"

"To make up for the fight we had, the fight that made me break it, she gave me hers. You mom is like that. I still got the doll, and never broke it. You done looking, Little?"

"Will you ever give mom's doll back?"

"I dunno. I guess it was a present, so I probably won't."

It was getting dark with the sky a net of sparkles, and they began to walk to the river together, remembering step by step. They heard the water rushing, and people singing along the main street of town. They climbed up the path to a point where they could see out, and the rocks were old men profiles, and groping hands, and wanting fingers. The wind came cold on the edge of it, and Margeen shivered.

"Auntie, I'm scared. It's dark out here, and ain't nobody around."

"It's dark out here. And there is nobody. Nobody. Nobody," said Franny.

It was like Franny was walking out somewhere on the rocks, and Margeen wanted her back, like when they ate the ice cream, and laughed at the boys, and like when she was solid and warm and grown-up, like she used to be.

"I'm scared too, Little, almost every day like I was your age, like wanting to be hugged and taken care of. And your mother, she doesn't understand yet, but I keep hoping she'll come back to me. But she's scared, too. It's like she's all the way across the water, and I can't get to her any more. I just want to tell her how it feels to be broken up, and to fit the pieces back into place. I've done so, so bad by her, going crazy, being a worry."

From where they stood they could see the deck and the flag of the riverboat down below.

"Can we see the boat, auntie, please?" Margeen said, tugging at Franny's sleeve. "Can we?"

They clambered down, and took the lower path down to the riverboat that was stuck on the shore under some heavy trees. They came up on a wooden platform that overlooked the ghostly Lady of the Dalles. If the band played at all now, it must have stopped, because they couldn't hear anything but the water and the creaking of the tree limbs. It was a straight, clearly lit path down onto the boat deck. Both of them hesitated on the top step.

"I don't like it, auntie, it's too dark here. What if somebody came?"

Franny looked nervously at the boat, which seemed to whisper stories about shipwrecks and wounds.

"Maybe there's ghosts, maybe the ghost of the Lady or something, auntie, I wanna go back."

And Franny quivered there like a heavy headed tulip in March, shook right in her shoes like a tulip on a skinny stalk. But there was something real stubborn about her mouth, and Margeen knew there was somebody on the boat and she knew that Franny was going down no matter. If Franny was going, Margeen was going too.

They silently took hands, and stepped down one step, and it creaked. One step became two, and then another, and then a whole flight down. They were on the deck in the bright lights. Careful like cats, they took their first step on the boat.

A lady walked out of the shadow of the prow.

Margeen couldn't scream, couldn't do anything but hold on to Franny. All her fear was at the ends of her hair, and she squeezed her eyes shut.

"Franny?" the lady said in an uncertain voice. "That you?"

Franny started to laugh so hard that it drowned out the playing of the band above them in town. Margeen opened one eye and saw her mother standing there just like always, in her jeans and sweatshirt. But mother's corn colored pony tail trembled just like the leaves on the trees.

"Where the *hell* you been, anyway, Franny, without telling me? I got half the county out looking for you! We been looking for hours and hours!"

Her mouth had taken on meanness, the mean that came out of pure not knowing what to do.

"Margie, we . . ." Franny began.

"No!"

Margeen's mother got it bad, she started walking up and down, up and down the boat, like she was going to pull all of her clothes to pieces, like she was going to jump in the river she was so mad.

"You don't get no more excuses, Franny, no more! I've had it with you, I've had it! I do every goddam thing I can think of, I worry out my life, *look* at me, I haven't had one good night's sleep since you got out of the hospital! Damn you, *damn* you, I wish you'd just be *decent*, I wish you'd just . . ."

"No!"

Franny said it almost exactly the same way as mother did.

"I got a right Marge, to be somebody," Franny sobbed out in a fury. "I got a right to be here, or anywhere *anybody*'d be. And if I'm not like I was before, then I got a *right* to be different than I was. I got a right to have a beautiful day, and you can't take it away!"

Margeen's mother looked like somebody'd knocked her down.

"I love you Margie, I guess you're the most important person in my life. But I came down here to see the river because I *had* to, and I got sick because I *had* to, and now I'm getting better because I *have* to. It never had nothing to do with *you*!"

Well, it was a picture, because Margeen's mother never cried at all, and she started to cry like crazy, and Franny started to cry, and so Little cried too, because other people's crying is so sad. Margeen wished with all her might that Franny would get better, and that her mother would get better, so that being a little girl wasn't so hard on a body. After awhile Franny hugged mother, and mother hugged Franny, and both of them hugged Little and said they were sorry for making her feel bad. It was funny how fast the sad all got over, and how the Lady wasn't so scary any more.

"Couple damn watering pots, you and me, Franny. Haven't cried so much since Willie Whats-His-Name dumped me for you back in junior high."

"Well, Judas, Margie, he was the cutest boy, and you treated him so mean that he treated me mean to make up for it after!"

"Wasn't so! And besides that . . ."

From crying to fighting to laughing they went, all the way back to town, holding together arm in arm in arm. Margeen thought she saw the big department store beacons making stripes in the sky and pointed upwards. Franny and Margeen's mother stared.

"Northern lights," said mother. "In summer. I'll be damned."

"It's a miracle," said Franny.

Margeen thought it probably was a miracle.

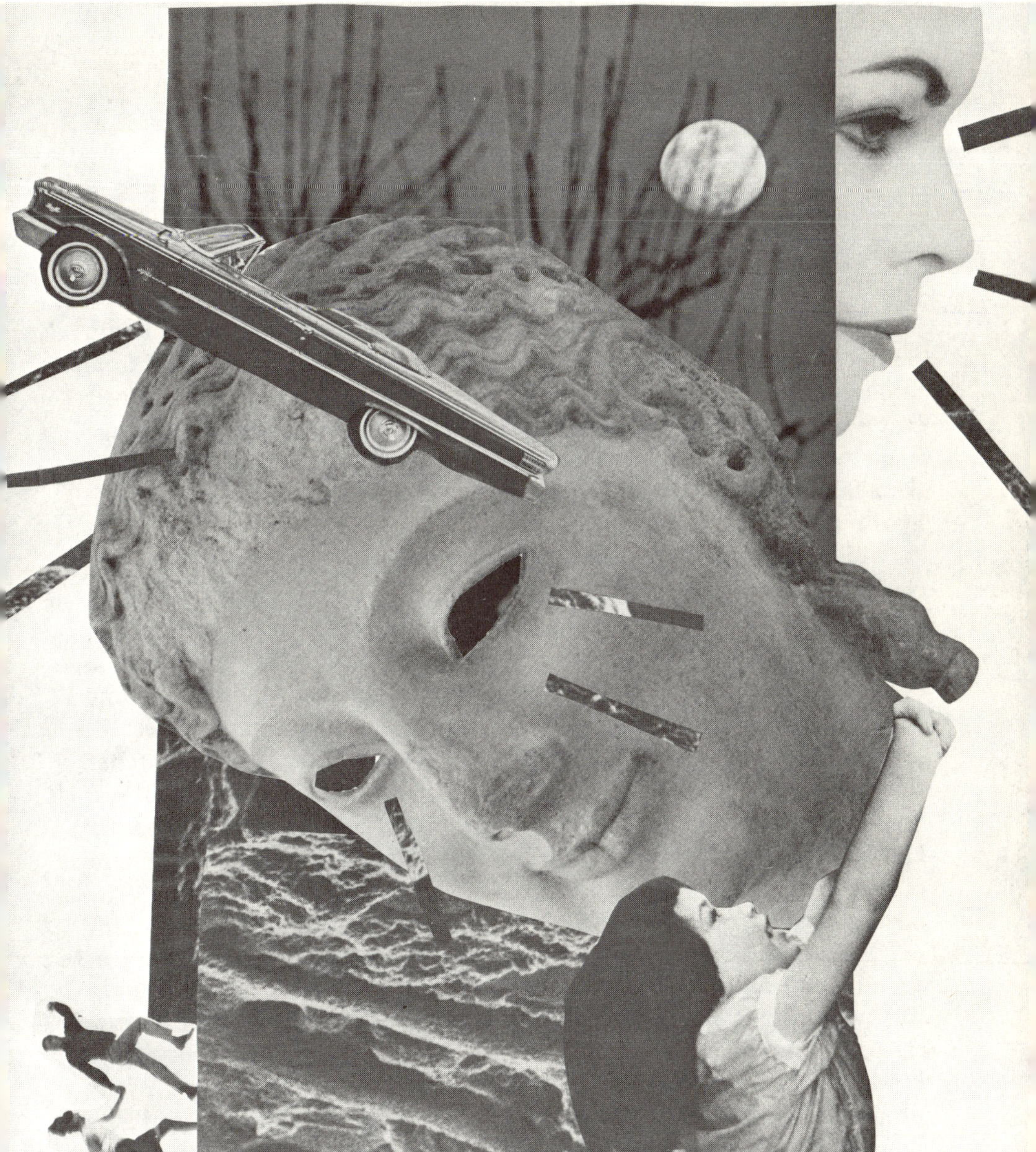

The Quidaxo Experiment

An Introduction to the Problem

THE SUBJECTS THAT THIS RESEARCHER was referred to were all union chemical workers, who had been exposed over prolonged periods of time to low doses of the quidaxo. None of the subjects were currently employed in the chemical field at the time of the study. They varied in age from twenty-seven to thirty-five. Two of the subjects were male, and two were female. I may as well give their names since I knew them quite well by the time it was all over.

Hovaness (hereto referred to as Subject A.) is now a stand-up comedian in Chicago, and has an unfortunate predilection for making jokes during assays and surveys, regardless of the serious nature of the research. Subject B., Catherine, is a very withdrawn individual, a housewife from Eden Prairie. This researcher had a difficult time restraining his finer feelings on several occasions when Subject B. showed signs of distress. In the cause of objectivity, this researcher admits to being somewhat taken with Subject B., who is a very regal and dignified blond woman, and who is unhappy. Second male Subject C., Keith, was going through psychiatric difficulties at the commencement of the study, and seemed impassive. The final Subject D., Victoria, was by far the most cooperative of the group, and seemed to have a temperment much suited to scientific investigation.

These people (or Subjects) were contacted by letter on April 4, and a follow up phone call and visit had to be made to Subject B. and C. before they were willing to become part of the group. Our facilities at the Mechanistic Research Center on Chemical Contamination were fully prepared for their arrival, and we received their previous medical files shortly before we met them. Two of them arrived by plane, one by car and one "on an ass, while lots of peasants waved palm fronds and called me Jesus Christ" (verbatim report Subject A.)

THE DESTRUCTIVE NATURE OF QUIDAXO has only recently been discovered and recorded in the literature. If we had known about its effects ten years ago, it is estimated that safety precautions could have saved over 500 union chemical workers from disability and death. All four of our subjects were unaware of the hazardous quality of the chemical, and all four were employed in a capacity in which they were required to handle quidaxo on a daily basis.

On the day of their arrival, we sat down in the Krutzwad Memorial Meeting Room to discuss the files of the subjects. I had a tape recorder and a twenty page summary describing what testing procedures would be carried out. They read these summaries quietly while I glanced over their files. The following information must be noted.

Hovaness, while working as a union chemical employee, was the least exposed of all the subjects, and therefore had nothing to report in terms of obvious problems. He claims that his excellent state of health is not due to less exposure, but to his Armenian heritage, which he feels gives him fortitude. His running commentary on things great and small, all of it ridiculous, seemed to irritate Keith and freeze Catherine, so that Subject D. (Victoria) was compelled to silence him on all topics (but she did it so tactfully, and with such an understanding of him, that I assumed that they must have been very close friends for some time.) Hovaness also showed overwhelming amounts of curiousity about the files of the other subjects, and when prevented from examining their records confessed to being "pathologically nosy." Subject Victoria then addressed some reflection to him on "the noses on these Armenians" after which she was cheerfully accused of purveying ethnic jokes. I thought it was rather funny myself, and it tended to relax Catherine, which was a goal of mine.

Catherine's file contained photos of the malformed child that she had delivered two years previously, and this researcher confesses to almost having lost his lunch when they were examined. She does have one normal son, and eagerly showed us a picture in a nice gold locket that she wore around her neck. Statistics on her engineer husband were also provided, and he sounds like such a very nice fellow that I suppose that I must give up all hope of her. Nonetheless, when questioned (gently, I tried always to be gentle) about her still birth, she began to cry in a thin hollow way, after which Subject Victoria put her arms around her and compelled me to stop asking stupid questions. I noted that while comforting Catherine, Victoria frequently used the word "partner."

Victoria had been a working partner of all. Catherine's exposure was extensive, and we expect that she may have incurred some genetic damage.

Keith's records were so fully explanatory of his mental health difficulties that I decided to add a psychiatric consult to the other planned testing. His exposure was also extensive, not because of his working in a high hazard area, but because of his carelessness in working with the quidaxo. During the entire interview, he said nothing, but he was taking anti-depressants and that may have been the cause. It is unfortunate that he has chosen chemistry as a career, as he, above the others, knows what his possibilities for damage are. I've tried to feel sympathetic to him, but he is such a squat morose lump of a person, that I gave up, perhaps too soon.

The maximum exposure was subject Victoria's. During my questioning of her, she sat placidly in her chair like one of those Campbell soup dolls I used to see other kids play with. She gave her marital status as 'living in sin', and has described symptoms which seem generally indicative of overwork. As the youngest and least educated of the subjects, I expected her to be the most excitable, but it turned out not to be so. I may as well note here that she seemed to be given the leadership position in the group, and answered questions that the others seemed to find too emotionally difficult. She demanded to read her medical charts every day, and to be kept in touch with the results as they were made available.

Her coworkers seem to agree that her manipulation of the drugs was the most professional. "We were good, but she was best." (Subject A. verbatim)

Materials and Methods

WE PUT THEM IN OUR NICEST ROOMS, the women in one and the men in another, although Hovaness complained about this type of segregation. He is a married man, and I didn't think well of his flirting with the nurses, but there—I always was a rather conventional person. We planned on keeping them for two days, and doing total genetic and physiological testing on them. They were fed on the usual 'hospital dogfeed' (verbatim, Subject A.). At first we decided to let them keep their own clothing, but this became impractical because every five minutes we were asking them to remove it. People are not supposed to look pretty in those abysmal gowns, but Catherine did. Victoria, on the other hand, looked much like a fat scoop of vanilla ice cream. The nursing staff noted that Hovaness's boxer shorts had obscene pictures on them, in fact they noted it so extensively that they had to be reminded of the serious nature of this project. Honestly. The kind of person that takes up nursing these days! It's debilitating.

We did a complete physical exam, genetic smears, blood and urine collection, and every other test under the fluorescent (see Appendix 1. for details.) A few times Catherine broke down, and once (to my very great distress) she began to cry for her husband. We eventually had to let Victoria hold her hand during certain procedures, notably the cat scan. The process took all day, and when it was over they were allowed to go out on pass and relax. It was when they returned that they informed us that Keith had gotten on a flight back without our knowledge.

I made some ill advised comment on our loss of a needed subject, and was firmly but kindly indicted by Victoria for insensitivity. I had the recorder on at the time, so I give a transcript.

"We're not subjects, Freddy, we're people. We're the ones facing sterility, genetic damage, and possible cancer, and *you're* inconvenienced? I don't know how you can look yourself in the face when you shave in the mornings!"

I was so sorry that Catherine had to see me in that light, and of course, Victoria was right. That night, after the others had gone to bed, I apologized to her, and she accepted graciously. It is to be recorded that Victoria suffered somewhat from insomnia during this time, and stayed up late to talk to me and the other staff memebers until three and four a.m. I found myself blurting out all sorts of very unscientific things about Catherine, because I was worried about her, and wanted her tests to come out all right.

Victoria told me that Catherine is, and always has been, a private person, and, alas, is very happily married. She advised me in a practiced way not to hope.

Results

I GOT MOST OF THE BLOODS BACK THE NEXT DAY, and found out exactly why Keith had taken off, poor man. He is a chemist, and must have known. But each of the others had better results than I had expected, better in every way.

It was found that Hovaness's sperm count was lowered, although he is not sterile. He surprised me by asking many serious and knowledgeable questions about aspects of the study underway. I am beginning to like him better, especially since he has taken a more protective stance towards Catherine. In fact, all of them have grown close, and for the human purposes (with which this investigation has no concerns) I feel it is good for them. After we get the last of the results, we can give him a clean bill of health. We score him positive for quidaxo contamination, as lowered sperm count is one of the documented side effects of the chemical.

My Catherine cannot have any more children, it was found, and this result dismayed her beyond what I have words to describe. There has been some stereotypic quidaxo mutation in oocytes. When I told her (why do they leave all the telling to me, my colleagues?) the three subjects congealed, glommed onto one another like antibodies, and hugged in their self-enclosed hazard. I was impelled to leave the room and use my handkerchief rather vigorously. For a while all discussion was at an end and the summation of Victoria's results had to be postponed. This was just as well, because the lab wished to re-do one of her blood tests. Her genetic screen was completely, almost textbook, normal. I somehow expected as much. Victoria is such a normal person.

Later, I have to admit, I told Catherine how sorry I was in terms more heartfelt than a good researcher is suppose to use. Catherine took my hand, and talked about my kindness, and spoke of her son in hopeful language. I believe she will be fine.

Discussion

All additional tests were completely free of abnormalities, and Hovaness and Catherine are going home. I will miss them, both of them, and although it breaks my heart to see Catherine leave, I send her away with the knowledge that is power. She seems to have adjusted to her news, and speaks of adoption. I am proud of her. I am proud of Hovaness, and admire his fortitude and good humor. Under less scientifically controlled circumstances, they could have been my friends.

We saw them off at the hospital door, Victoria and I. Victoria leaned against the doorframe in a way that made her look almost tired. She was again delayed because further tests were asked for. My colleagues told me that the lab kept losing her samples.

"I'd like to go and see Keith when I get done," said Victoria. "I think it would be fair."

"I loved her, you know," I responded, watching Catherine drive away.

"We have a lot in common, Really, safety is nothing. All of life is hazard."

"I hope I see her again someday."

But then I noticed that Victoria was crying, the kind of tears that sort of slide out of wide open eyes. I asked her why, that being the human thing we do.

"Oh, Freddy, can't you see it? I've known it for weeks and weeks. For God's sake, can't you see it? It was an experiment in human life, and I've become a percentage, and can't you see that Catherine at least gets to walk away alive?"

The lab results came back. Victoria was sent to oncology that afternoon.

Conclusions

A THOROUGH TESTING WAS DONE on four subjects, all of whom had been exposed in their occupations to the toxic chemical quidaxo. Of the four subjects, Subject A. had a lowered sperm count, for reasons unknown. Subject B. had genetic damage in oocytes, because of chemical exposure. Subject C. did not complete the process, but what testing has been done indicates carcinoma of the bladder with metastases to the brain. Subject D. has leukemia.

They tell me that Victoria is going to die.

I never expected science to be like this.

A Brief Encounter between the Barracuda and the Last American Virgin

HE PROWLED THE BLUE LIGHT BAR like a barracuda in a bird bath. Eyes met, turned away, returned to him, to appraise his black hair and sleek body. He measured and calculated girlish bodies, womanly bodies, elegant bodies. Bodies were his specialty, his calling, his rationale for being in the bar. All the numbers in his book bored him, all the familiar lines were too familiar. He was looking for something different, something ornate for the jaded palate. He knew that he would find it there.

Sometimes he wondered what made up his facination with the place. It was a low down, loony, dirty, young honky tonk in the middle of a staid city. The loosest and the youngest could be found and had for nothing in the place. Young. Maybe that was the drawing card. He'd grown up in a generation that hadn't trusted anyone over thirty. He was over thirty, and didn't trust himself. Sometimes he like to roll and grovel in his own failure to be happy, by picking out the young and worthless, any little girl, every little girl, who was going nowhere fast, and not planning on taking him along.

Burnt offerings tonight. On weeknights, it was drunks and cocaine burnouts, chemically treated self-abuse machines. From the brassy blonds in barely adequate halter tops to the painted models reeking decadence of bygone eras, he has seen it all before, had it all before. He would have it again, if nothing better presented itself. But he was looking, always looking, for something not even he could define.

Loud boogie man blues rammed the gut and set the drunk to dancing. He looked down the line, saw faces that melted into one another and into the smoke. Then he saw her. She was looking right at him and smiled something human from across the room.

I'm a man, he thought, a human being for once. He went to her slowly, although he would have preferred to run in threw opposite direction.

"Hello," he said.

"I wasn't sure if you'd remember me," she responded.

She hadn't changed much. She'd never been pretty, and she still wasn't pretty. Her hair was still unkept, her upper lip still had an eccentric bend, and if she'd changed her clothes in three years, it would have been a surprise to him, because she was wearing the same thing.

"How could I forget?" he smiled. "You never were one of my success stories, were you?"

"It depends on what you mean by success. I'm glad I made a dent, anyway."

"Is that what you were trying to do, leave a dent?"

She considered this, in that flightly abstracted way she had of considering things.

"Yes. I think people should leave dents in you. I think if they did, you wouldn't be so bored all the time."

"Love is a many splendored sting?"

"Love? I don't think we ever talked about that," she said. With a naive and trusting air she then asked: "Are you going to ask me to fuck with you again?"

He laughed, like it hurt him, uh-uh-uh, like a gramaphone winding down. She could have been asking him about the weather.

"I've jumped the convention, haven't I?" she giggled. "But you understand, don't you?"

"Does it matter?"

"No, and if you knew how long it's taken me to say that, you'd sing the Marseillaise and buy me a beer."

"*Can* I buy you a beer? Someplace where I can hear what you're saying?"

"As long as it isn't your apartment, and as long as you at least hum in the parking lot."

They struggled to the door. On the way there, some sweaty young man in a tee shirt pinched her ass, and she stomped on his instep. About ten feet from the door's slit of yellow light, the barracuda began to hum the French national anthem.

******

"...IT ALL TURNED OVER, I guess. A couple of things. When I was in New York, waiting for my flight to Paris, I went into one of those pay toilets and took the non-pay booth. On the back of the door, some woman had put a survey about virginity. You were supposed to mark how old you were when you lost it. Mostly, people marked down seventeen, eighteen, nineteen. But there was a clump of people in the late twenties category. It's nice to be in a clump. I didn't feel so much like a freak then."

They strolled around the bathtub that was Lake Calhoun, dodging the lovers and the midnight joggers.

"Did you ever think about me there? I know that must sound egocentric."

"No. I never did. Before I left, I thought about you a lot."

"You blame me for not calling you again after that last night?"

"Blame?" She puzzled over this. "No, never. It would have been so easy for you to seduce me. Not doing it was about the kindest thing you could have done."

"Kind." He looked for the word in the water.

"Yes, kind," she persisted. "Don't you think it was?"

He melted into the grass, smelled the algae that was blooming in the muck by the shore.

"I had a wife once, and a son. My wife was as good a woman as they make, but she wanted me to be faithful, and I couldn't be. I drove her out every time I came in smelling like somebody else, until one day she just wasn't there. When she left, she was already gone. My son calls me up once in awhile, trying to connect with me. He needs to find out what I am so he can find out what he is. I tell him I'm busy. I don't want to waste the time. My only sister died last month. I didn't go to her funeral. For me she was already dead. My uncle gave me a good job at his trucking outfit, a management job. I lost it. It was too much work."

"Change," she said, throwing her hands up, showing him the cloudless night.

"Never."

A nightbird wheeled close, called out in desperation, and disappeared.

"Even refusal has an integrity," she said sadly. "I know."

******

IT WAS TOO LATE TO GO BACK to the bar. It was too late to call any of the multitude of numbers in his book. It was too late to do anything but go back to his sensually arranged apartment and drink. He paraded them in his mind, the women he could remember, a lovely parade. Usually this variation on counting sheep put him to sleep, but tonight the effect was the exact opposite. He closed his eyes, listened to the melancholy jazz trumpets in his stereo speakers, until it internalized. He then picked up his phone, dialled his newest number, and spoke softly into the mouthpiece.

"I can't live any other kind of life," he said. "I can't live any other kind of life."

Doing the Ark Solo

THEY PLAY THEIR SILLY SNEAKY TWEAKY GAMES in the front seat, boring, boring, boring. They speak French to each other, not even knowing or caring that I understand their fussy dovey whisperings, purposefully excluding me from the tight circle of their mutually enlightened relationship. The third wheel, the fifth horse, the spare female tire: Love thy neighbor, but only if she belongs to somebody, only if she can entertain herself by drawing condensation pictures on the rear window of a compact automobile.

Venom. I've got more poison than a basket full of copperheads.

"No, don't worry about me. Just let me out at the corner," I tell them.

I used to have a sense of humor about other people in love.

******

"YOU'LL MAKE IT, DANIELLE," Ben remarked in slimy tones of abdication. "Go out and find some nice guy from the mate-for-life school. Consider me a long introduction."

"Say it more clearly, Ben," I said. "Say it so I can hate you, okay?"

He sighed. Passions exhaust him.

"Blue jeans and wire-rimmed intellectuals went out with the hippie-dippies, Danielle. You're a little dinosaur. I feel like a jerk when I take you to a party and everybody else has clean hair and Calvin Klein tatoos and nice manners. Your working-class ethics are a drag. Some people grow and some people don't. You haven't."

"I'll change!"

"You can't. Rocks are rocks and trees are trees. Give it up, Danielle."

Am I the rock or the tree? I've been trying to figure it out for a month. I'm afraid to hold a pen or say my prayers until I know which.

"Let me out on the corner," I tell my two friends who rescued me from the night, this night. "I only live across the street."

******

It was pre-ordained that i should have this breakup point of view. I was coupled to Ben early in my life, in our freshman year of college in fact, and so I always saw the world in couples, animals marching into staid marital arks. Pregnant women see other pregnant women, parents tend to note other parents in crowded shopping centers, old women of similar backgrounds gravitate together by laws of nature on buses, bigots find bigots, fools find fools. Now all I see are people with faces empty and wistful, floating in the created seas of their lovers' rejections, while the ark floats by.

In bible class, I recall hearing that Noah sent a blackbird out into the obscurity before he sent the famous dove. The blackbird never returned. Its mate had to do the brave new world solo.

Did I fly away into the fog, or did Ben? Questions all of the time, too many questions.

******

Ben is making his mark in the world, on both trees and rocks. He didn't used to be ambitious, I was the ambitious one. With blind partiality, I believed that society needed only to see him to worship him. Every vacuum in his perfect persona was filled by my efforts. In college, I wrote his papers, then I wrote his resumes, then I wrote his grants and proposals, all to carefully reflect what I knew his ideas to be. It never bothered him that he was functionally illiterate. It never bothered me either. I was wrong, and he loved me wrong.

But I really would have changed, I would have!

"Are you sure you wouldn't like to come over and have a drink?" my friends ask me gently from the front seat.

"No. I really would like to be alone, thanks all the same."

I climb out into the snow, my back stiff from the cramped rear seat. They just look at me, uneasy, unwilling, unable. It might happen to them tomorrow. I hurl myself into the little cockpit, sweep my lips against their cold cheeks

"I'm better now, really better," I cry.

"We're sorry," they say.

******

Actually, my friends have all betrayed me. Venom.

At first, I waxed confessional, weeping about the terrible way I had manipulated Ben's sensitive free spirit, and had used him to accomplish what I was afraid to attempt. They agreed. Then I poured out vitupertion on the expedient bastard who sponged up my soul and took away the Waring blender, which was a mutual gift. They agreed. Nobody wanted to dispute either point of view. Nothing is more boring than someone dumping their love puzzles on your rug night after night.

My friends have tried to moderate me, deflect me from my obsessive harping on the subject. They take me out to dinner, and propel me to movies with hidden messages. Then they kiss and touch one another, ignoring me, their duty fulfilled. Their intimacy is the wheel and the rack. I tried to express this to one of my friends. He got angry, and told me he wasn't willing to be miserable for me, thank you very much.

"You built it all yourself, Danielle," he said. "I care about you, and I feel bad for you, but I'm not willing to spend my life going doom-doom-ker-doom just because you and Ben broke up."

I remember crying. Almost continuously, in fact.

"Look, honey," he said quietly. "It's happened to me. You get over it. Take a little time to adjust. There is life after Ben."

Prove it to me.

******

THIS IS ACROSS THE STREET. I live here. Every object in this room is exactly the way I left it this morning. I look around, trying to logically evaluate the differences between the rooms of a single woman and the rooms of a coupled woman. Well. There are three days worth of dirty dishes in the sink, victims of my apathy. There are fewer mirrors. There are no athletic tube socks draped over the lampshades. The half-finished paper in the typewriter is mine. I try to look at all this sensibly, and I'm having a terrible time.

The phone rings, I know it is Ben, just as I've known it was Ben any one of a hundred times since he moved out of this place. I run to pick up the receiver.

"Hello?"

"Hi, Danielle! It's Nan. How are you doing?"

I'm crumbling into a million pieces.

"Oh. Not so bad. What are you up to?"

"Nothing exciting. I thought I might come over and tell you all the unsavory gossip I've collected this week. Care to indulge?"

Everybody should have friends like mine.

"C'mon over. Only how do you feel about dirty dishes?" I say.

"I live my whole life with them. What of it?"

"I've got a collection here that would disgrace my mother. I think I'm backsliding into individuality."

"It's about time."

******

CAN I BE BOTH, THE ROCK AND THE TREE, solid and changing, the mate who sails off into the wind, the mate who waits, can I be both? I found the naswer last week in an old can of shaving foam that I found on the shelf in the bathroom cabinet. I sprayed a globule on my hand, and I couldn't put it back. How does the stuff get in there in the first place, anyway? I'll never know.

He called, of course, called too late, after all the questions had become more intriguing that all former intrigues. His colleagues had finally discovered that Ben couldn't put two words together. Olive branch, he chirped. Dry land.

"I need to talk to you," he said winningly. "I need, I need, I need."

Quoth the blackbird.

"Ben, I'm telling you. This doesn't float in the water," I say.

I may be wrong. But I can't be wrong forever.

Jasmine's Mother

ON MONDAY, MRS. NORTON, THE FIRST GRADE reading teacher at Kincaid Elementary, gave a short lecture to her students about debilitating conditions, and how nice children do not harass their fellow students who possess them. None of the first graders understood how to pronounce debilitating condition, but they did know when they were being chewed out for doing something wrong.

"I think we can't be mean to Millie any more," said one little boy at recess. "That's what."

"She's wimpy," snorted Harvey Bollinganger who, because of his name, had a reputation (deserved) for picking fights. "She's funny in the head."

"Mrs. Norton says she's ela-pha-leptic, and it ain't her fault," sighed Lisa Stewig, remembering with equal guilt and fondness her yanking of Millie's long black braid only the day before.

"Should we ask her to play kick ball?" James Franklin III asked.

"Shit, no," said Harvey. "She can't play nothing. And who knows when she's going to have a fit? And it'll get blamed on us. But hey. Where's the new girl? Did she run away or something?"

"I'll bet she's afraid, cause she don't know us," said James.

"Not her," sniffed Lisa, the femme fatale of the junior set. "She's just stuck up, is all."

Harvey, thinking he'd like to get to know about the new girl, searched the grassy playground of the elementary school for some sign of the bright emerald jacket she always seemed to be wearing. He finally saw the new girl, crouched on the ground on the pavement circles where ball games were played. He could see her short coppery curls above the collar.

"Over there. C'mon."

Harvey, Lisa, and James hustled over to the circles, and only slowed when it occurred to them that the new girl wasn't alone. Millie, a horsey looking brunette with ugly standing out freckles, was bent over the thing the new girl was showing her, her face alight with an absorbed intelligence.

"Hey!" said Harvey, who didn't know other ways to enter private conversations.

The two girls looked up, Millie in panic, the new girl with some evidence of displeasure. Harvey thought she was awfully small, this new girl. She was tinier than every other girl in the first grade, and had delicate china skin, aqua blue eyes, and hair the color of copper pennies.

"Hey yourself," said the new girl. "Come and see."

They came. In front of the girls were a collection of odd looking metal pronged bits, and a bright orange ball.

"It's a game," said the new girl. "You have to be pretty fast to play it. You bounce the ball, and while it's up in the air, you've got to scoop up the jacks, bingo."

She did it for them, first picking up one, then two, then a handful, as quick as they could blink.

"I never saw that game before," said James. "Is it new?"

"No, it's real old. My mom taught me to play it," said the new girl, and her face lit up with a smile as she said this. "It was what she used to play when she was like me. I guess they didn't have Space Invaders then."

"I can do that. Lemme have them," demanded Harvey.

"I'm teaching Millie today. I'll teach you tomorrow."

"Now," said Harvey. "Or I'll take 'em away and bury 'em."

The new girl, whose name was Jasmine, gave Harvey a long look of recognition. She didn't touch the jacks. She stood up, took Millie's hand, and began to walk away.

"Hey!" yelled Harvey. "I want to know how to do it! You can't just walk away!"

Jasmine turned around. Her lips were shaky.

"You're a bully, Harvey. My mom told me there was a bully in every crowd. She told me not to fight a bully. She told me to walk away and have dignity. She says bullies never have any dignity. So you can steal my jacks, if you want, but you can't make me show you how to work them."

"I do so have dignity!" said Harvey, hurt. "I just want to do it now."

"No. I'll show you tomorrow. Today, I'm playing with Millie, because she has seizures and you're mean to her."

James and Lisa knew it was a showdown. There was no doubt who was bigger. Or who had dignity.

"Okay, okay," Harvey said with grudging respect. "Tomorrow."

Jasmine smiled.

"Okay yourself," she said, trembling with relief. "I know how to play marbles, too. And I have baseball cards. Do you have baseball cards?"

"Do *I* have baseball cards?" Harvey said, smugly strutting around Jasmine. "Is the Pope Polish?"

In this way, Millie and Jasmine became integrated into the group at the private elementary school. The tiny redhead was a cinch at marbles and card games, but Harvey could beat her at sports events, so he didn't lose too much face. Millie was deemed acceptable after Jasmine pointed out that she could fold her eyelids back, and was double jointed and could do funny things with her fingers. Jasmine's definition of epilepsy was a bit more comprehensible to children than Mrs. Norton's, also. She explained it, via her mother, as a switch going off in Millie's head that made her nerves go haywire for a few minutes. It all began to sound rather romantic to the kids, and they had practice seizures until Mrs. Norton made them stop.

Jasmine entered into all activities of the school with verve and goodwill. Nobody had a better disposition, and few of the children were better liked but it was Lisa, her nose out of joint by this loss of attention to her own small person, who began to point out that there were some odd things about Jasmine.

For one thing, she always wore the same clothes. She had two pairs of overalls, one green, one blue, and she wore these every other day. They were always mended and clean, but had patches on the knees. On warm spring days she wore the green jacket, and on rainy ones an orange yellow rubber raincoat with a peaked hat, but she had only one pair of shoes, Stride Rites of oxblood red with loose soles. She always brought her own lunch in a beat up metal Superman lunchbox, and it was always the same lunch—a peanut butter sandwich, an apple, and a cookie. The cookies were always homemade, though, and had fancy decorations on them.

Jasmine frequently mentioned her mother, but never her father. There were lots of children at Kincaid with single parents, so this was not unusual, but most of the childrens' single parents had jobs, and Jasmine's mother didn't seem to. Also, Jasmine didn't know anything about TV or movies or videogames, and could never follow the others as they discussed the plot lines to their favorite shows. Nobody ever picked Jasmine up at school, not her mother or her father or a nanny (some of the wealthier kids had these), and nobody came to the PTA conferences for her. She walked the block over to Lincoln street and took the city bus home every day. The children began to realize that Jasmine was probably poor.

"Like the Waltons," said Harvey, whose father was a lawyer for the county attorney and divorced from Harvey's mother. "It's too bad. I bet they don't have any lamps, and use candles and stuff. Maybe we should ask her over to our houses for TV."

But Jasmine wouldn't play after school. She went right home every day. Harvey thought it was probably because she had to do chores, only he didn't know what kind of chores people did in apartment buildings.

"Well, what d'ya do all the time at home?" Harvey asked.

"Mom and I do the envelopes. She types on the front of them, and I put the papers in, and lick them. And mom and I read, and play games all the time."

"Where do you live, then?"

It turned out that Jasmine lived on the West Bank, which was where everyone knew the hippies lived. Harvey's father had told him that.

"Is your mom a hippie?"

"I don't think so," Jasmine said pensively. "I'll ask her."

She came back the next day, and told Harvey no.

Did Jasmine's mother play bridge? Harvey persisted. Did she play raquetball at the club like Harvey's mother? Did she shop at Lunds? Did she drive a car? Did she gamble in Vegas? Did she have a boyfriend?

"Nope," Jasmine replied to all. "My mom doesn't go out of the house. She takes care of the plants, and cooks dinner, and does the envelopes. She just be's my *mother,* Harvey. She seems pretty happy. We have lots of fun. We go out at night sometimes, and go to the Riverside cafe if they have music, or we go walking, and on Sunday we go to church."

Harvey entered into a sort of Jasmine fantasy life. His mother was a weekend once a month, too many chocolate sundaes, a series of boyfriends who all had good tans. He tried to imagine what it would be like to have a mother like Jasmine's, who read to you, took you to the Riverside cafe at night, baked cookies with smiling faces in the icing. He saw her loving, mild Mrs. Walton face, with tendrils of reddish hair coming out of a bun at the nape of her neck, bending over to straighten his collar, fluff his hair. From his dream, Jasmine's mother began to affect his life, gentle him, resolve him to higher and greater purposes. All he had to do was watch Jasmine for a example. She never hit, never yelled, was never mean, and took her turn at games without complaining. Harvey still beat up on anybody who gave him grief, but because of Jasmine's mother, he began to feel bad about it, and want to change.

"I'll bet your mom's beautiful," Harvey said wistfully. "My mom is, boy oh boy. She's a fox, But I bet your mom is pretty like a mom."

"She really is," said Jasmine.

Then came the year end roundup, when all the first graders and all of their parents got together for a carnival, with food, and free pop, and reports, and plays, and displays. It was required for all parents to come, and Harvey's mother consented to go, even if his father 'that bastard' was coming, too. Harvey's cup flowed over. Not only would his parents (who had split up, of course, because of Harvey, as Harvey well knew) be together for once, but he'd get to see that saintly paragon of all the homely virtues, Jasmine's mother. He was so caught up in rapture, that he didn't notice how quiet Jasmine had become, and how nervous her eyes were.

"My mom's bringing a chocolate angel food from Lund's," said Harvey to the playground crew. "What about you guys?"

"My mom and dad are on the committee," said Lisa importantly. "They arranged the pop with the Coca-Cola company. With the *president* of the Coca-Cola company."

"Paper plates," said James darkly. "And napkins."

"How about your mom, Jasmine? Is she gonna make those neat cookies with the animals?"

Jasmine looked at the sky, at the ground, everywhere but at the kids.

"I'm bringing a cinnamon pound cake," she said. "From my mom."

"But, she's coming isn't she?" sputtered Harvey.

"No," Jasmine was facing it out. "No, she can't make it."

Harvey exploded.

"If she was any kind of mother at all, she'd come! Even *my* mother is going, and she doesn't even *like* me! I think you're a liar, Jasmine. You probably don't even have a mother. She probably hits you and drinks whiskey and..."

Jasmine barrelled into Harvey with the full force of her anger. The two children kicked and scratched at each other, tussling on the ground, and even when pulled apart by the teachers they spat and snarled. They remained in opposite corners for the rest of the afternoon, and went home in opposite directions.

Harvey felt bad about the fight, but worse about his mother dream. He decided to call Jasmine's mother, and tell her how important it was (for Jasmine's well being, of course) for her to come to the roundup. The first time he called, he got Jasmine and hung up. The second time, he got a strange slurred deep voice with a gurgle in it. The voice sounded drunk. Harvey knew what drunk sounded like. His own mother was very often drunk when he called her. Harvey hung up, went down the basement, and pounded on a four foot clown punching bag his father bought him. Now the Jasmine's mother dream was different. Now she was an elegant, lolling redhead with too much makeup, asking little Jasmine for a refill.

The next day was the day before year end roundup. As soon as Jasmine arrived at school, and put away her lunch box, she walked up to Harvey. Hard task was written all over her face.

"My mother talked to me last night." She launched into this statement breathlessly. "And told me I had to say I was sorry I hit you, and she *will* come tomorrow and she will bring the cake herself, so there!"

The next night, Harvey's father picked up his mother at her apartment, and they all sat together not talking. The Lund's angel food was on his mother's lap. She glittered in the darkness, her dyed blonde hair in fashionable cascades down her back.

"What an ordeal," she yawned.

"Ellen, the boy," said Harvey's father.

It was always the same, and it was always bad. Harvey looked out the window.

The gym was set up like a carnival, with games in all four corners, food tables in the middle, and balloons strung from both basketball nets. There was a conference corner for the teachers and parents, and to Harvey's dismay, his father went there directly, leaving him alone with his mother in this place where she didn't want to be. He and his mother dropped off their angel food among all the home baked goods, and got a free coke at the fountain machine.

He never knew what to say to his mother. She was twitching, and examining her watch.

"You want a smoke, don't you mom?"

She deposited a smile in his lap.

"Dying. Simply dying for a smoke. Never mind. I can go through it just this once, for you."

"I'm sorry you have to be here," he said bitterly. "I'll never ask you again."

The mother bit her lip and shrugged.

"No, dear, it isn't like that. I do want to see you but, you see, this isn't my scene. I'm really fond of you, Harvey, but it's so hard trying to pretend to be what I'm not."

And suddenly Harvey was blurting it all, about Jasmine's mother, his dream and his disappointment. As he looked up, expecting to see the mask of displeasure his mother put on when he broke or spoiled things, he saw tears in his mother's eyes. She knelt down in front of him, and ran her laquered nails through his hair.

"Oh, Harvey. If only you could understand! I was always a failure at mothering. It just isn't my style, never was. I wish you wouldn't take it so hard..."

Then Harvey heard Lisa screaming, and a couple of the other children yelped, and ran to their parents in fear. The whole auditorium full of people stilled as a pair of figures made their way shyly into the auditorium with halting steps. Harvey gripped his mother's sleeve and his teeth chattered.

"Mom, mom..." he said, pointing.

"Don't be afraid," said his mother, with a tremble between a gasp and a laugh in her voice. "Remember your manners."

It was Jasmine, in a dress of green velveteen with lace, obviously made by clumsy hands for the occasion. She was beaming, beautiful, a tiny star. Her flaming curls were tied up in a pained bow, and her oxblood shoes were spit polished. She was holding hands with a monster, or so it appeared to Harvey.

Harvey didn't know at first whether the thing were woman or man, but it was thick and hunched and twisted. It had short iron grey hair, and wore a polyester pant suit of navy blue and no other ornaments. One of its shoulders was higher than the other, and one of its feet dragged as if it hurt the thing to walk. Its right eye was directed at the ceiling, and its left at the room. A massive scar linked its eye to the corner of its mouth, giving it an evil grin. The hand that Jasmine held had two fingers missing, but the other one was thick and blunt and strong, like a man's hand. Harvey looked away from the thing to his mother.

"What is it mom?" he whispered.

"Jasmine's mother, of course."

Harvey saw that Jasmine's head was tilted up proudly, and she smiled from head to toe. She was happy and honored to be seen with the thing. Mrs. Walton died a natural death.

"It's horrible," said Harvey.

"It's wonderful," said Harvey's mother reverently. "She isn't ugly to the little girl, Harvey. And don't you do any acting out, you hear me?"

Lisa was a hysterics, and had to be taken out, but the other kids began to mill around again as the two dropped their cake at the table, and Jasmine introduced her mother to the ladies of the PTA who were taking in the goods. Mrs. Franklin II, James's mother, offered her hand to Jasmine's mother, who took it and shook it as if she thought if was a pump handle. Jasmine spotted Harvey, waved, and led her mother in their direction.

Harvey felt a scream coming up inside of him, and was about to let go of it, when his mother stepped forward, insouciant, graceful, and offered her manicured hand to Jasmine's mother.

"Ms. Bates? I knew it must be," Harvey's mother said in her gay bright voice. "How do you do? I'm Harvey's mother. Please call me Ellen. And you, young lady, must be Jasmine. How do *you* do?"

"I do just great," said Jasmine, wrinkling her nose at Harvey.

"Hi," said Harvey to Jasmine's mother's good eye.

"Hello, Harvey," said Ms. Bates in her curious slurred voice.

"Gee, isn't this just great?" Jasmine enthused. "The balloons are neato rikito. Can I get a coke, mom? You want one?"

"Go ahead, dear," slurred the monster tenderly. "Nothing for me." The two kids danced away, leaving the mothers facing one another.

"You have a beautiful daughter," said Harvey's mother.

"Yes. Yes."

Jasmine's mother bent her head humbly before the lovely blonde, and she was crying.

"I tried not to come. I never should have come."

"You think not?" Harvey's mother took Ms. Bate's arm and began to promenade with her around the room. "Look at your child. Why, she's floating on air! You're the queen of the May, Ms. Bates, and really how formal that sounds, what is your name?"

"Bernice."

"Then, Bernice, I've been convinced that you're a paragon by my son, who I assure you greatly admires you. Now, lets sit down over here and get cosy. I'll brag about mine if you'll brag about yours, and we'll be disgustingly maternal together. It ought to be a new experience for me, God knows."

Bernice Bates stared at her daughter, who was socializing with a vengeance.

"From the day she was born," she said. "Purely a miracle."

"Lucky, lucky you! Lucky Jasmine."

While the parents held conclave, the children were also exchanging their views.

"Harvey, your mom is a knockout. And so classy!"

Harvey looked for a tactful thing to say, and couldn't find a one.

"How long has she looked like that?" he demanded.

"My mom? Oh, before I was born. She got into an accident in a car. It made her back funny, and it hurts her sometimes just awful." Jasmine leaned forward confidentially. "I'll tell you another thing. She gets kind of sensitive. Some people get funny around her because she doesn't look like other moms, but I try not to let her know about that. It would hurt her feelings, don't you think?"

Harvey had to admit that this might be the case.

Parents and children got rounded up towards the end of the evening.

They sang God Bless America and saluted the flag. The family units collected together, and filtered out. The two mothers, ugly and pretty, said their goodbyes.

"It was an honor, 'Jasmine's mother'." said Ellen. "Please have Harvey over, won't you? Your daughter has a civilizing effect on him, and he does need taming!"

"You're a good woman," said Bernice. She tried to smile, but the weaker muscles of her face couldn't handle it and it kept slipping off to one side.

"Ah. Debatable. But I quarrel with no compliments. Thank you."

As Harvey and his parents left, Harvey heard Jasmine's voice, a golden bell, from across the room.

"Mr. Phillips, hiya! Have you met my mom?"

The Harvey contingent was in the car before the smile fell off of the socialite's face, and she sat in the bucket seat of the car and cried.

"Mom, what's the matter?" Harvey said. "You did great. I was proud of you."

"So was I, Ellen," Harvey's father remarked, surprising everyone.

"Oh, you're right. I'm acting like a ninny. I should never let myself get involved in anything touching. Harvey, don't you think your Mrs. Walton types are a bit of a bore?"

"Have a cigarette, mom. It'll be fine."

"You little beast!" she said, laughing. "You deflate me every time. Yes, I will have a cigarette, dammit, and I won't go all melty and apologise to you, Harvey, for being such a lousy mother."

"No, don't do it, mom," said Harvey, who finally did understand. "It wouldn't be your style."

The House of Wong One

THE HOUSE OF WONG ONE is wedged between a tire factory outlet store and a Little General quick stop. It is as small as is Wong himself. As Amit and I walked up the cracked concrete steps in the misty rain, my muscles tightened with a desperate pleasure. I had worked on Amit for a long time to get him to make this concession, to get this chance to label him in the eyes of the world as mine. The party would be brimming with his friends from the department, the friends he had tried to prevent me from meeting for so long.

It took a great deal of applied psychology to back him into an invitation. His reluctance conjured suspicion in me, forced me to consider the possibility of another woman in his life, but the charm and sweetness of the invitation, once extracted, was enough to dispel my worst fears. Perhaps I did go to extreme lengths to bring it off, but I can be very touching when determined. Knowing him so well, I avoided protests, arguments, scenes. Instead I faked melancholia, and wept a little bit, accusing him of being ashamed of me. Amit never resists such persuasions, Still, I sensed an underlying turbulence beneath his elegant front which did not promise a comfortable night.

"This isn't a very nice neighborhood, is it?" I asked.

Amit shrugged irritably.

"Wong hasn't much money. Poor people must live where they can."

"Of course. I think his story is very sweet. I hope he can afford to send for his fiancee in Hong Kong soon. I really intend to like him, and all your charming friends."

His black eyes flashed once in the lamplit curtain of mist.

"Not all my friends are charming, and not all the people here are my friends. Gossip is their primary occupation. For my sake, will you be careful?"

"Your interests are my interests, darling," I whispered.

I had dressed with particular care that night, in a simple dress of black silk that stated my respectability, my status as a lady. When one sleeps with a man on weekends, one tends to be seen in a certain way by low minded types of people. Amit and I agreed that we would be 'just friends' for the evening. I wore my most decorous silver earrings, sprayed myself subtly with Joy, and polished my nails with particular care. When we left his apartment together, we both looked magnificent, he a picture of foreign elegance, I a sobered Christmas angel. No one who saw us together could call us badly matched.

The back door opened to us, and we stepped into the gay light-filled house, and were greeted with warm murmurings and laughter. Wong One immediately popped out of the haze. I knew him by his miniature size and his legendary Hawaiian floral shirt.

"Amit. You are late. We have started without you," he said.

"I got delayed," Amit responded. "Wong, I would like you to meet a friend of mine from Milwaukee. This is Diana. Diana, Wong One."

Wong's eyes shifted from my face, to Amit's, to mine again.

"You are welcome in my home," the little man said cautiously. "Please enter. Have a drink."

Frankly, I was disappointed in him. From Amit's description, I expected a much more respectable sort of person. As Amit's best friend in the department, Wong One should have been impressive, powerful, influential, but he was in fact nothing by a dirty little Chinaman with a broken accent and uneven teeth. Resolve stiffened my smile. If it were up to me, I would have Amit move in only the best circles. I intend to have him finally, and it is not too soon to begin building him into the man I want.

People filtered in, and I felt a bit overdone, but people are my medium, and I charmed everyone I could get my hands on. I found myself nodding brightly while people bantered about their tedious pharmacy jobs, their real estate deals, their dogs and children. It was hard not to yawn at times, but I managed it all superbly. While threading my way to the kitchen to pick up another drink, I heard one man say to another:

"That Amit. Some guys have all the luck."

"The blonde? Yeah, what a knockout."

I saw my triumphant eyes in the glass of a china hutch, when I heard this comment:

"Yeah, he has a way with the ladies, all right. Wonder what Emmy Lou will have to say about it. She's got it bad for Amit."

"Oh God."

Emmy Lou. It sounded like one of those tacky countrified names, like Betty Joe or Bobby Sue. Her name spoiled my enjoyment, as all my suspicions came back again, made my drink taste flat. People tooted horns, smoked, drank, and I redoubled my efforts in every part of the room. I wanted to get those people accustomed to me, to know my name as the really important one.

I was standing in the hall politicking with Amit's direct supervisor, a superior individual, when a woman arrived. The wind practically blew her in the door. Well, she was unattractive, in a way that I particularly deplore. She was skinny, and rangy looking, with messy brownish hair, and harsh pseudofeminist glasses, and big horsey teeth. The coat she wore was eccentric, but rather nice. I decided to condescend to her.

"Oh, what a lovely coat!" I exclaimed.

"Gee. Thanks," she smiled, as if I'd given her a rose, poor thing. "I sort of like it myself. It's the only classy threads I own. Is that Cynthie laughing in there? It always sounds as if someone were tickling her feet."

Verbose, to top it off, I thought. Her voice sounded offensively decided and unfeminine. I smiled vaguely, tiring of the charm lessons. I was looking for the mysterious Emmy Lou, not some bumptious girl in blue jeans.

"I hope these heavy drinking types left me a beer or two," the warm fuzzy female remarked, while pushing up her glasses. "You're an awfully pretty one. I don't think I've met you before. Do you work in the department?"

"No," I replied, only half engaged. "I work in Milwaukee. I'm a friend of Amit's."

"Oh," she said.

"You've dropped your nice coat," I pointed out helpfully.

"Oh. Thanks, yes. Me, I'm naturally clumsy. What did you say your name was?"

"Diana."

"Pleased to meet you. I need a drink, is it that way?"

"Right in the kitchen. But you haven't told me your name."

"Oh. Sorry. Name's Emmy Lou."

I didn't understand at all.

"But are *you* the one who works with Amit? I mean, I think I've talked to you on the phone, haven't I?"

"Yes. I'm the one."

She was the one. I watched her slide into the kitchen. I saw Amit's face light with recognition when she entered the room, and saw her elbow past him. He turned to offer some joke to her, but she turned her back, without speaking. It was rude, and I was glad of her rudeness. There was a sinking in my heart, but with it a surge of almost vindictive triumph. I could defeat her instantly. All I needed to do was stick close to her, and let him make the comparison. It would be child's play. I was alone in the hall, and then not alone. Wong One had materialized behind me.

"I will tell you a story, pale haired lady. You will hear it," he said.

He was called Wong One, I was told, because he got drunk on one of anything, and I could see he was drunk now. The print in his offensive shirt made me dizzy. I made a motion of distaste.

He launched into the story, regardless.

"Once upon a time there was a little boy, who had a skill of catching spiders. He would take two of these prizes together, and put them in a bowl, and fight them for the amusement of the other little boys. This made him greatly envied by his friends, as he had no other skills . . ."

"I don't know if I want to . . ."

"One day, he captured two very fine ones, brave ones both. He called together the boys to watch. And the spiders approached one another in the bowl. But instead of grappling with each other, they made friends. Together they climbed over the rim, and ran away into the grass. The boy was made a fool. He caught them both again, and put them into the bowl, again and again, until, tortured to their limit, they both jumped on the boy and bit him. It is the only way in which some people learn about spiders."

I ran away from him. He was frightening me.

"You don't have to play his game," Wong called after me drunkenly.

They were together. Amit had cornered Emmy Lou, and the crowd kept them in the center of the room, over the baskets of crackers and plates of cheese. I could see her trying to escape. Now was my time.

"Hello, you two! Amit, why don't you go and get me a drink, there's a darling, and I'll drag all the gory details of your work habits out of this nice woman?"

Oh, was he uncomfortable. I didn't even care. I was intrigued. What part of my image-conscious lover could possibly be interested in this lisping rag with the Charlie Chaplin face? It was a part of him I didn't know.

"So tell me," I began. "Do you like the department? To tell you the truth, Amit often finds it boring."

"It is boring. But is pays me a living wage."

"You're not a student, are you?"

"No," she paused and, somewhat cynically, continued: "I have no great ambitions."

"Well, I'm finishing up my master's degree in psychology at the University of Wisconsin. I have a seminar here on weekends, so I come every Friday night to stay with Amit for the weekend. He must work very hard. He's always so tired when he comes home to me."

She winced as though she'd been kicked, but summoned up a smile that even I could not have managed under the circumstances.

"Yes. I suppose. He's trying to get over. They're grooming him to take an administrative job, I hear. Me, I'd rather relax and enjoy life."

"People who relax never go anywhere."

"Yes, they do. They just do it slowly, and like themselves more when they arrive."

"How do you have opinions about it? You say yourself, you're not ambitious."

I knew that would get her. I knew it.

"I did say that," she responded, her face softened with something almost offensively like sympathy. "I meant that I'm not ambitious in the way you are, or the way Amit is. I don't need to become somebody. I am somebody. To my family, I guess, and my friends. To these people here. Sometimes I forget that, but that passes off soon enough. Now, I guess I want to be happy. To learn to be happy. When you finish your degree, will you be a psychologist? Will you counsel people?"

I found myself talking about my program, and about my reluctance to deal with all those desperately scary crazy people they make me deal with in my clinics. She threw questions at me, one after another, until I'd forgotten who she was and how I was supposed to feel about her. She knew my field, enough to ask right things. We both continued to drink, and she pulled out of me opinions, fears, thoughts that I have about my work that I've never voiced before. I felt as if she were looking into my heart and talking to the part of me that knows I am a dilettante, that knows I want to marry and quit worrying about the horrors of deeply troubled minds. Throughout, she was sickly pale but self possessed, in a clinical sort of way. I liked her against my will. She said some of the rudest things I'd ever heard, and charmed every snake I own. Finally, I stopped talking. I was tired as I haven't been for years.

"Look at Wong," she laughed. "He's passed out on the stairs."

He was, and yet he wasn't. I felt as if he'd been listening to me expose my mortal soul, although he couldn't have been, really.

"He's odd."

"Wong knows where the bodies are. People don't pay much attention to him, except to have fun with him, but Wong knows all and tells none." She looked at me shrewdly. "He's a prince. Cultivate him. You have the knack."

She got up, and set Wong's tipped over beer bottle on the floor. Her fuzzy hair momentarily brushed his cheek as she kissed him. It made me feel ashamed of myself, to see her do it. I discovered the spider story again. The way she touched him was antenna sensitive. She then turned to leave.

Around the room, people were casually watching her go, just as they had watched us talking together for that hour. The challenger, they would say, had gone down in quick defeat. I did not know whose defeat took place, whether hers, or mine, or Amit's.

He intercepted her at the door.

"Are you leaving already?" I felt curiously detached about him then. His face contained no love or even liking for her. He looked more like a child whose favorite toy was broken.

"Yes. And well I should," she replied.

"I'll punish you for this, for leaving my party so early."

She looked up at him. I knew the look in her eyes as I knew the look in my mirror when doubts overcome me, when I sense the smell of another woman on his skin, when I know that he will never commit himself to me, when I know that he keeps me around for the sake of convenience, when his eyes are distracted with the dope rings we blow around the bedroom. I heard a tinkling sound over my shoulder. It was the splash of Wong's broken bottle, whose tender brown shards glittered under my elegant pumps.

"I asked you to come especially," he tried again. "There will be dancing later."

She looked over his shoulder, met my eyes, then stared over me. Wong One was wide awake now, as impartial as an icon.

"So? If you want to dance, dance."

She was out of the door and gone. He turned, and his brows snapped together as he saw me. Was he registering me as an enemy? Chagrin and irritation made him look sulky, much younger than he was. He came up and sat down beside me. I put my hand over his fondly, out of habit I think.

"This is such a nice group of people," I remarked in false-bright tones. "Your friends are so pleasant."

"Yes."

Wong One tapped me on the shoulder, as if to remind me. What, he seemed to say by touch, if the two combatants are worth more than the prize? Sitting before me, staring forward with a thwarted look, I almost thought Amit looked rather shallow. But he is so incredibly handsome. His exterior and mine are so equitably matched.

"Darling?" I tried.

"Let's dance," he said aggresively. "Let's dance."
I'm determined to have him. I love him madly.
We danced.

A Christmas Card for a Mother

IT HAD BEEN MAKE, AND SCRAPE, and contrive, and now it was all over. She collapsed at the kitchen table which was littered with paper and bows. The big packages had to be wrapped in the funny papers, but the kids wouldn't mind. It was only adults who worried over the surface. Kids cared more for the substance.

She hauled boxes and bundles over to the tinsel adorned tree and methodically began to arrange them in artistic piles, almost lingering over the task. Here was Mary's sled, Louise's new doll, Gary's handsome plaid robe, all carefully chosen by her own hands. She gave an extra caress to Albert's new sweater. Her husband would probably take it back. Lousy bastard, she smiled to herself, while rearranging the bows.

On impulse, she turned on the lights and the tree awoke, a warm entity with a life of its own. Sitting back on her heels, she observed her own handiwork. It was a bright Christmas card for the sandy eyes of waking children.

"What a maudlin thing to think. But I do..." she whispered out loud, "...feel like God on the seventh day."

For a few moments she existed in the present, impervious to the aching in her arms and legs, impervious to the exhaustions sweeping away the nervous energy that had kept her going for the last few days. The lights absorbed her, pulled her in, reflected her face. They began to blur. Let the wolves howl at the door, goddamn it, let them dare, she thought. However poor we are, I can still make Christmas for my kids. The look on her face was fierce and protective.

This emotion also passed, and left behind it a sudden sadness. The muffled movement of sleeping bodies was all she heard. It was so lonely, up late alone, even in one's own house. Sometimes she craved silence and privacy, and like most parents of small children, would often have killed for the chance to simply read a book all the way from beginning to end. But now, it seemed like she should be able to share with someone her accomplishment. The world is always asleep when I want it, she mused.

Shaking her head, she got to her feet and began making the rounds. The girls, angelically tousled on their twin beds, were sighing. Gary, her oldest, was arguing baseball with an unknown umpire. Baby Jamie was a plump pink bundle, and his mouth dribbled on his sheets. In their own room was Albert, flat on his back, with his hands folded corpselike on his chest. She never liked to watch her husband sleep. She almost felt relieved when he woke up every morning.

Restless still, she walked about the living room, picked up the spare wrapping paper, emptied a few ashtrays, looked out the window. It was snowing. The stars rang cold bells in the sky. The glitter called her out to dance, to hide, to make magic. For a moment, she stood as transparent as glass, and the night blew through her like the north wind.

A half an hour later, the door of their small apartment silently locked behind her as she tripped off into the white glow.

******

THE CHURCH BEAMED WITH YELLOW LIGHT and poinsettias, and the strong voices of the eighth graders in the choir loft made young and heavenly music. She was late, and dipped a genuflection before quickly settling into a front pew. Midnight mass, a rutual from her girlhood days, enveloped her. The church was cold, and she snuggled deep into her old tan cashmere coat. She had, for some unknown reason, decked her own halls with all the small clothing elegancies that she had salvaged from her previous unmarried life. Anyone would have taken her for a slight and delicate young girl, with her slim calves and her correct little hat. Even her face belied the fact that she had four children sleeping peacefully in their beds.

A few of the parishioners around her smiled at the earnestness of her responses. "Peace be with you!" she almost shouted out loud. She sang the hymns in a high clear voice, slightly off key. "O rose from root of Jesse, from whence the Lord has sprung. It bore a flower bright. That blossomed in the winter when half spent was the night."

******

FILLED WITH AN INNER PEACE foreign to her turbulent nature, she listened to the sermon, only hearing those words that struck harmony with her mood, drifting in the warm commonality of the ceremony. On the long walk home, she sang the chorus of the Gloria, and laughed without cause. She ran up the steps and swirled gracefully into the house, smiling out loud.

She found her two daughters with their heads hung, amid a pile of shredded paper, their hands holding those things that she had so much wanted to see them open. The surprise was spoiled beyond mending, and packages were thrown garishly around the room. The cherished picture of her children joyfully opening her gifts of love dissolved. Whatever kind of light had been struck in their faces at the sight of their new and fine things was lost forever. All she would see, for a year's contriving, was this timid fear.

"Go to bed. Right now. Don't say one word."

"But mama, we thought..."

"*Right now*!"

They scrambled away, frightened, not understanding. Tense, in their beds, with the room dark, they heard her turn out the lights. They fell asleep while listening for her to move, or breathe, or even cry, but there was nothing.

And in the morning, they peeped around the corner. Their father and brothers were unwrapping their gifts, joking and laughing, and their mother was laughing, too, with her teeth clenched. There was a breakfast with French toast and real meat sausages and fresh squeezed orange juice, like they almost never had. They saw that she had dropped a sprig of holly on every plate.

And if it broke her spirit, that mother, and if it took all of her self control to pretend, and if she never forgave her daughters but tried to, then it was more than anybody ever knew, because she never said anything but Merry Christmas.

The Chaplain Miscarries

I LEFT A NOTE AT THE NURSING DESK the day the Chaplain's baby died. It took the nurses and me a while to come to an agreement on who the note was going to because their records said "Gena Winiarcyzk" while my internal records always register "The Chaplain." The confusion was resolved when I impatiently told them I was talking about the *chaplain* Gena, the student minister.

"Ahhh," the nurses sighed sadly. "Ahhh."

Gena was still in the delivery room when I left my note, getting some kind of drug that is supposed to hold back inevitable abortions. I asked to go up and see her, but they wouldn't let me because friendship is not an official position. For all they knew I was just another curious gossip, wanting to buzz an interesting story around the hospital where she and I both worked.

"I'm a close friend," I told the head nurse. "Could you please page me if anything happens? I'm the house orderly for the oncology wing, my beeper number is..."

"Why don't you just check with us tomorrow?" the nurse said tepidly. "I'm sure we'll know the outcome tomorrow."

"Can I leave a note?"

Dear Chaplain, You'll do anything to get out of work, won't you? Relax, drink all your fruit juice, and for once in your life, do what you're told. We'll get through this. I'm behind you 100%. Love you.

The nurse took the folded note, opened it briskly, and read its contents while I shifted from foot to foot. She looked me over. There was nothing much to see. I was dressed in my whites, white jeans, an India bazaar cotton shirt, white tennis shoes, tinted pink glasses. My hair was growing out from a bad dye job and a worse haircut. My fingernails were laquered in passion purple and I probably wore too much lipstick, well, I suppose I did look like something out of central casting.

"So why are you reading my note?" I complained.

"I just wanted to make sure that you didn't mention anything about babies in it."

"Is she going to lose the kid?"

The nurses lips tightened, and she said nothing.

The note got to her the day after the baby died, after Gena had held it in her arms and given it goodbye. It was a small white slice of eternity, less than two pounds, perfectly formed as a statue in marble, a little boy. The very nurse I talked to left Gena and her husband with the baby for several hours, or whatever the accepted medical time for grief is. During this period the real hospital minister came in to see them. He found them alone in the darkened room. I was waiting for him when he came out.

"I don't know why I went into this line of work," he said. "I don't know why, but it looks kind of different when it's one of your own. She had such a mission, such a mission..."

He began to walk away from me.

"What do you mean, *had*?" I asked.

"You'll see," he returned, without turning.

They didn't take Gena back to the station where I left the note. The women on that station have babies that survive birth, and are generallly happy about that. The Chaplain couldn't go back there. Instead, she was taken to the minor surgical ward with all the appendectomies and tonsilectiomies and other-ectomies that constitute removal of unwanted parts. My note made its way to her by other channels, its ambiguity made it acceptable. She was still refusing visitors, but she was receiving written communication, or so her husband Dillman told me.

"She put it into the bedside table with other sympathy cards and stuff like that," mumbled Dill bitterly. "You should read some of them. 'God works in mysterious ways', and 'It's the Lord's will', and even a whole passage from the book of Job."

"How is she taking it all?"

"She cries a lot. Excuse me, I've got to get to work now, I'm late."

"But Dill, I really think I might be able to help if I could just talk to her."

"Marta, look," Dill took hold of my shoulder and shook it. "She needs gentle people now, she doesn't need any grief, she doesn't need any cynicism, she doesn't need any of your damn sophistication. Let her get stronger some. You told her you care, that'll be fine, just leave it be, okay?"

I shrugged, and walked away. I suppose I deserve Dill's rejection, and Gena's, but the idea just nagged me, of the Chaplain surrounded by soft kind Dill, and her soft kind mother and father, and her soft kind minister, not to mention all the medical staff people, who go all soft and kind whenever anybody dies. It was a sixth sense, a Gena induced sense, a sense that resulted from my conversion, that told me that the Chaplain needed me. She used to lecture me all the time to open myself up to feel the needs of others, to work at being a real Christian whatever my religious beliefs, to maximize and sensitize. I used to find that pretty contemptible, in a beautiful way. Then the contempt melted and the beauty remained. Nothing really changed but my anger, which suddenly became unsavory, and I felt that I owed it all to the Chaplain. I remember fondly every argument we ever had, and they were numerous and explosive, but none was ever as bad as the one we had about her pregnancy. We'd cut communication for six months over that one, and I suppose that Dill felt that now was an inappropriate time to straighten things out.

So did Gena's mother. I went to the quiet funeral service for the dead baby, and finally saw the Chaplain. She was standing with her back to the winter sun, staring down at the floor of the church, her straight tan hair quivering on her shoulders, her hands two painful fists. A weak beam of light strained through colored glass fell across the breadbox sized coffin with its meager decorations. I was absorbed in the scene, when I heard a voice over my shoulder.

"Excuse me."

"Yes?"

"Would you mind very much not coming to the internment," Gena's mother hissed, while fingering the gold cross on her neck fiercely. "I'm not sure darling Gena is capable of coping with any difficult personalities."

"I guess I can understand," I whispered, tears stinging my eyes. "Okay. It was just that I...never mind."

It was then that they turned, the whole party turned, the service was over, the breadbox in black moved slowly down the aisle, Dill took the Chaplain's arm, and I finally saw her face. It was petrified wood, the ashy color of people naked in the cold, but her eyes burned with a possessive fervor as she watched the little box floating away on a sea of stained glass light. As she walked by me, oblivious to my existence, I dropped my prayerbook on the hollow wooden pew. She saw me, stopped. Dill's face accused me from behind her shoulder.

"I haven't been crying," she said to me quietly. "I wouldn't give him the satisfaction."

"How d'you know that God's a him," I responded automatically.

I always used to bait her orthodoxy that way, and she always used to laugh.

She turned away from the casket and back to the altar.

"I won't give you the satisfaction," she said softly, then the next sentence boomed out like the scream of a woman giving childbirth. "Your love is a lie, it's a lie, a bloody lie!" She kept on screaming until those concerned relatives of hers smothered her into a faint. An usher took my arm into custody, and I was led out like a miscreant blasphemer. The Chaplain's mother told me, in no uncertain terms, to stay away from Gena. I was shocked at the results of my actions to the extent that I finally decided to take her advice.

Gena called me two days later

"I'm tired," she said. "I'm tired. Why don't you go away when you're making me tired all of the time?"

I didn't know what to say.

"You wanted me to fail, didn't you? I want you to know that I understand how much you wanted me to fail. Can't face me? Why don't you come over here, you cowardly...witch!"

She always had trouble getting out cuss words.

"I'll hit you, you just come over here, and I'll tell you every ugly thing you're afraid to hear. Dill is gone. He won't protect you. I dare you."

"I'll be over in fifteen minutes."

I hung up the phone, and got into my car. I'd just gotten home, and still wore my whites. My old Vega backfired down Lake Street, it coughed and spat and abused me. One of its headlamps didn't work, so that the whole nighttime road was vertigo slanted. I pressed my foot down hard, zoomed around an obscenely decorated van, and narrowly missed a cat that didn't know any better than to prowl on the road.

Her building is one of those plastic ones, where all the walls are carted in by a big truck and dropped in place, and the corners are puttied up. I could hear children everywhere in the building, and smelled the smells of people's dinners, and the smells of monthly roach poisons. I knocked on the door, and a voice told me to come in. The lights were dimmed. The Chaplain sat on the floor. In front of her was an amazing collection.

It was a tiny trousseau, a department store of knitted and crocheted wear, little pink socks, soft square blankets, mountains of cosy sleepers, rattles and bottles and stuffed doodads. Gena was wiping her eyes with an ice cream colored bootie. As I stood with the harsh hall light framing me, I saw the face I didn't know dissolve into the one I did know.

"You're standing like a John Wayne movie," she said.

"Quit making jokes, Chaplain, and cry your fool heart out. What the hell's the matter with you?"

She started throwing soft kind little clothes at me, I was being powder puffed all over by mittens and afghans, and she was screaming at me those few curses that she knew.

"I hate you! I hate."

Then the barrage stopped, and she collapsed into a puddle of released emotions, I knelt down with her, and held her, we rocked and rocked. I think I would have sung a lullabye, if I had known one.

"He was perfect," she sobbed. "He was pretty, his hands and feet were just perfect, and I wanted him so bad."

"He's dead."

"I felt him kicking me, moving inside of me, just a few days ago. When I held him, he looked like he wanted to open up his eyes and talk to me, tell me what it was all going to be like."

"He's dead."

"He was going to be an artist, he was going to speak seven languages fluently, he was going to be the next liberal chief justice of the Supreme Court, he was going to change the world!"

"He's dead."

"But when they took him away, I knew that if I'd only done something..."

"There was nothing you could do."

"I failed him, I must have done something bad to myself, I tried so hard to be good, I worked too hard, I ate wrong food, I didn't pray enough, it was my fault..."

"No," I said, rocking away. "You know that isn't so."

"But it was my body."

"You were born with one body, and if it didn't work exactly right in one circumstance, so what? It's the body you were born with. How could you help that? There isn't any way you can accuse yourself. He died, the doctors told you why he died, it was unavoidable. If anything could have been done to save him, you would have done it."

"I really would have." She leaned against me, exhausted and restrained. "If anything could have been done, I would have done it."

"Right," I said. I thought I had the thing done.

"It was God. I'm being punished by God."

I pushed her away, and energetically started putting all the creamy little outfits back into a box that was laying in a corner. The Chaplain went into the kitchen to pour herself a cup of coffee, a beverage that she had forsaken for despised fruit juice when she discovered her pregnancy. She sat and watched me dump item after item in the box.

"It was just like you said." Gena was as relaxed as a cat now, enervated by spent passion. "If there's some higher power, it's probably negative power. We really are just animals, being jacked around like pull toys for cosmic amusement."

"So since when did yours truly, old tough shit Marta, become a world authority?" I held up the ice cream colored bootie to the dim light. It looked like it had been dipped in stained glass.

"Do you know why I helped all those patients at the hospital? Because *I* needed to. Social worker chaplain Gena, bringing the holy word into the sickrooms of the nation. When I think of the number of people I sent away praising the goodness of God, I want to suicide myself. You were the only one who knew what a hypocrite I was."

"You gave them something."

"Lies. You told me how people are. Since I lost the baby, my eyes have been opened, everybody is so cruelly kind, so sweet and empty, so full of spiritual consolation. I didn't fail, and God is good. Lies."

My conversion was delivered to the church door with no clothes on, it didn't wear a religious affiliation, it was a husky little heathen with a tough exterior and the Chaplain midwifed it. She had changed me into a better woman without my ever feeling any pain. I didn't realize that conversion worked both ways. While Gena was teaching me to be patient and tolerant I was teaching her to be cynical. It was supposed to be my conversion, how could I know?

"That was why you kept saying all of those terrible things to me, about how little Dill and I could afford a baby, about how children complicate lives, about how stupid I was to get pregnant before I even knew very much about the world, naive, that was what you called me, innocent, stupid Chaplain. Well, you were right. I never want to have another child, I never want to want anything that much again ever."

It was the shadow over her face. It had to go.

"Did it ever occur to you that I raised all those spectres of parenthood because I didn't want you to be happy?" I demanded, cruelty in place. "Did it ever occur to you that I didn't want you to have anything that I didn't have? I knew that namby'pamby 'faith' of yours was nothing but a blind. One crisis happens in your neatly ordered life, and whammy—all of a sudden you cry out against your higher power and, in the same breath, try to blame yourself for failing some kind of test. If you were rational, not so much of a religious fanatic, you'd realize that you'd had a miscarriage, after which you'd be kind of sad and angry for a while, after which you'd go have another kid. But not you. You've got to get it all tied up with some grand design. I tell you, I feel like a big success, now you're as cynical and guilt ridden as I am. So you know that people are 'like that'? Well *I'm* like that, too, and it's about time you faced up to it."

I didn't even know what I was saying. I only knew I wanted it to hurt.

"Get out of my house," Gena said quietly. "Get out of my house."

We used to talk about sudden trauma, the Chaplain and I, especially in the context of hospital patients. She always went for the nice kind approach, but I never learn anything from nice people. Shock treatment is about the only thing that works for the heavy-duty beliefs. Dynamite has lots more power than stained glass windows. I left Gena's house, and I haven't seen her since that time, it's been about six months now. But...

I found a note in my mailbox one morning. It was not addressed to me, but I knew that I'd been beaten all hollow for brevity on notewriting. The paper held only two words: *You failed.*

The next day I made up a package for Gena containing a can of her most detested fruit juice, a coupon for a dollar off disposable diapers, a pair of fuchsia punk baby booties, and the names and room numbers of two patients that I knew who needed to talk about loss. It was not long afterward that I found out the the Chaplain was pregnant again, and that the ministry was in operation everywhere but my wing.

There was something funny that happened, though, that I don't understand. I found the names of the two needy patients in my mailbox today, with another brief note written on the bottom.

Talk to them yourself. Love, the Chaplain.

Meeting the Interface

SHE IS LEGITIMATE, I swear.

The child is, the child I toddled up and down the men's clothing section of the department store, while her mother inspected slacks. I was only pretending, playing a game that many single women play with other people's children. For a few moments, I was mommy, leading my fantasy daughter Nik-Nik from rack to stack to pile.

She greatly prefers things tactile and geometric, this pretend child of mine. She likes to touch the bumpy walls and bury her nose in 'fluffies and shaggies' socks. I let her touch everything. Being a fake parent has its advantages: Discipline is someone else's duty.

Her age is fifteen months, and she is supposed to have fifteen words at that age. Nik-Nik has seventy-three words (I counted once) and the most commonly used two are What Dat? Certainly she is a prodigy. Also, she is beautiful, with skin the color of coffee with lots of cream, and downy brown eyes. Her fuzzy brown hair was pulled into pigtails and decorated with candy-colored barrettes that day. Trundling along the crowded aisle in her bright blue overalls, she kept pointing excitedly at the Izode Lizard.

"What dat?"

"Lizard. Can you say lizard?"

Unfortunately, no. She went through her repertoire briefly: she, toes, socks, baby, daddy, mama, Em'ly, frog, woof-woof. No lizards had yet crawled into her baby garden. We explored further.

"What dat?"

She pointed at the flower arrangement, coyly I thought.

"You know what that is. You tell me. What's that?"

"Flowers!"

She beamed, and then sniffed the fake blossoms on the plastic plant. I patted her on the back, and was considering leading her back to her mother, when I heard her take in a long raptured breath. Her center of gravity is low and she managed to plow her way through the umbrella and silk-tie underbrush between the counters before I was aware. She waddled up to a woman with a stroller stuffed with a newborn baby. The woman had two shuffling children dragging mournfully behind her.

"Baby!" Nik-Nik gasped happily. "Baby!"

The two children stared, and their mother turned away from pricing jockey briefs. The mother looked at the cafe-au-lait Nik-Nik and then at me, while the clerk over her shoulder tried to catch the preoccupied Nik-Nik's attention by putting a pair of red briefs on top of his head and grinning like a clown. I giggled. The clerk giggled. The mother turned coldly to the clerk.

"I'll take them. Put them in a bag."

I suddenly realized that the temperature had dropped, and put one hand protectively on Nik-Nik's head.

"Cute kid," the woman muttered, when she could see that Nik-Nik wasn't going to budge from her rapt adoration of the baby.

Nik-Nik grasped the front bar of the stroller, and cooed at the squishy pink bundle packed into it like an egg in a styrofoam carton. One of her pudgy tan hands gently reached for the face of the sleeping infant.

"Baby," crooned Nik-Nik. It was salute and caress.

"Cute little pickaninny," the mother said uneasily. "But could you get her away from my..."

Nik-Nik softly, ever so tenderly, patted the infant's cheek.

The woman yanked back on the stroller.

******

IN 1968, EMILY FERGUSON WAS FOURTEEN years old, and had just been transferred to West Metropolis High School because her father had just taken an engineering job which paid him enough so that he could afford suburbia. Before then, Emily had attended Our Lady of Peaceful Endeavor grade school. Emily was sheltered. She had never heard a black person called anything worse than a Negro, mainly because there were no blacks at Peaceful Endeavor in 1968.

There were two blacks at West Metropolis in 1968.

One of them was Samuel Washington, the son of a general practitioner and a high school home economics teacher. Samuel had no interest in medicine or home economics. He wanted to be a policeman and arrest arsonists. Since Samuel was imbued from birth with a great deal of Christian fortitude and stood six foot four when he was fifteen years old, he managed to graduate on the B honor roll, and got a football scholarship to the University of Minnesota, Duluth. There he distinguished himself in sports, lounged cheerfully through a criminal justice degree, and joined a crime prevention project as an assistant director when he graduated. He married, and led a respectable life. Emily Ferguson used to run into him once in a while in shopping centers, and they would mumble hellos to one another.

The other black person was Corinna Frasee, the daughter of a widowed heavy equipment operator for Bingo Construction Company. Cori had no interest in heavy equipment. She wanted to write for the *Minneapolis Tribune*. After struggling unsuccessfully to become a reporter on the high school newspaper (the West Metropolitan) she took to sending freelance pieces to *Seventeen* and *Tiger Beat*, and eventually got in print. Cori graduated at the top of her high school class, took a journalism degree at Columbia, got married and divorced once, worked her apprenticeship on the Walasengo, Minnesota *Beam*, and was finally hired as a reporter for the WCAB television news team. She can now be seen three out of every seven nights on the ten o'clock report.

By coincidence, Samuel and Cori and Emily were all new to West Metropolis High School in 1968. There were a few other teenagers at West who were new, but Samuel and Cori and Emily were all living within a few blocks of one another, rode the same bus, had the same study hour, shared the same classes their first year, and were all against the Vietnam war. This last fact alone made them fairly unusual at West, which was a decidedly 1950-ish place in 1968. That all three held this opinion in opposition to their parents made the possibility that they would not become friends remote. They became friends.

In 1970, a race riot broke out on Falmouth Street, in the poor section of town, and for several days police battled rioters, who burned down businesses, abandoned buildings, and (occasionally) their own homes. Many people were injured in the riots, but nobody was killed, and it quieted down within one week of the initial explosion. None of this happened anywhere near West.

Three of the businesses that were destroyed in the Falmouth Street riot (a liquor store, a second liquor store, and a furniture liquidation outlet that had a large side door marked: AFDC orders taken here) belonged to people whose children were students at West. Six buildings that were burned down belonged to absentee landlords whose children attended West. A small band of Westies comprised mainly of children of injured property owners decided to take racial matters into their own hands. Since Samuel was a big strong teenager who played on sports teams to the glory of West, it was decided that he would escape retribution. Cori, being smaller, female, and bookish, seemed like a more likely candidate for being taught a lesson.

So, on her way home from school one afternoon with Emily Ferguson, Cori was seized upon by a group of these young interested citizens. While the male counterparts held her, the female counterparts bloodied her nose, tore her collar, rubbed dust in her hair, and one of the boys pissed on her shoes. Cori went home in tears, alone. Her father took out his heavy equipment (he was a large individual) and went to talk to the parents of the ruffians. The parents of the ruffians promised to chastise their children, some of them actually did (but those were mainly the ones into chastisement for its own sake), and it all eventually blew over. There were no more race riots on Falmouth Street, and no more at West Metropolis. The most devastating result of the Cori-attack was that Samuel quit the basketball team and West lost the district championship. To everyone's great disappointment, a romance never budded between Cori and Samuel, and consequently they stayed friends for most of their adult lives.

When the revengers attacked Cori, Emily had screamed at them then, when threatened, had wavered, then had broken and run. Cori and Samuel, being practical children in their own ways, considered this act 10% betrayal and 90% self preservation, and treated Emily accordingly. However, since guilt was much of what they taught at our Lady of Peaceful Endeavor grade school, Emily never forgave herself for running away. She grew away from Samuel, and tried to grow away from Cori.

Cori had other plans. She was not exactly innundated with prolific offers of friendship, and so discovered early that good friendships ought not to be sacrificed to the noble guilts of religion. After trying to be encouraging and comforting to Emily, Cori decided that Emily was not susceptible to niceness under the circumstances. In frustration, Cori, after a one sided argument with her friend, hit Emily over the head with an ancient history text. This gentle persuasion seemed to free Emily from guilt enough so that the two could re-establish their relationship.

So the two women grew up together. Emily watched Cori marry again, this time to a reporter on the *Minneapolis Star.* Their marriage was good, and they had one daughter who they named Nicole, but who was called Nik-Nik by just about everyone.

One day a small incident happened while Emily was watching Nik-Nik for Cori, and Emily had a re-occurance of guilt.

This is what this story would look like if it were being written by an objective person.

The woman jerked away the stroller, and her baby woke screaming, while Nik-Nik fell on the plush carpet of the department store. She tumbled in slow motion, balancing precariously for a moment, then losing it, ending up on her pudgy hands and knees. There is always a few seconds between the surprise of the fall and her cry. The mother snapped "Sorry!" while her eyes narrowed with anger and embarrassment. She turned her back on me and mine.

"Hey, that was lousy!" yelled the clerk, still with red shorts hanging over one ear. "Whatya think you're doing here?"

I said nothing as he yelled after the mother. I scooped up Nik-Nik and heard the infant screaming at its parent as the woman wheeled it off into another world.

Nik-Nik stopped weeping soon, and submitted to being carried back to her mother, Cori. Her verbal flow was not free. I didn't want to pretend to be a parent anymore.

"Good baby," I crooned to Nik-Nik. "Good girl."

"Mama?"

She sounded subdued, she needed the real thing.

"Mama?"

She is legitimate, my Nik-Nik. She cries instinctively on meeting the ugly interface. It is I who stand aghast in cold white silence, not saying what I know, not acting, not being, pretending, guilty, always running away away.

Uncle's House

HER UNCLE'S HOUSE WAS BEING BURIED NOW, and Mali had to see. When she took off her scarf in the entryway to Malone's Funeral Home, the electricity in the knit made her dyed blond hair stand out, as if her whole head was frightened. Terrence gently smoothed her hair. The spark he made on touch contact made Mali jump.

"Hey, babe," Terrence said. "Remember me? I'm the man you wake up with."

"Sorry. I'm really sorry," Mali replied nervously.

"Relax." Terrence squeezed her playfully. "You look great in black."

Mali did look good, she'd always needed to. She bought a dress for the occasion, a modest one with long sleeves, and a high neck to cover up the paper wrinkles beginning to form at her throat. It could not make up for her wild past, however. All the relations would remark on it later, while standing around the coffin like a Greek chorus: Thirty-five and not married. Thirty-five and been around. She wore her hair unsuitably young, lined her eyes carefully, and pressed makeup into the deeper lines, but Mali was still thirty-five and not yet settled into that most desired of lifestyles, marriage. The relatives always thought there was something a bit strange about it, a bit secret.

"Are we going in, or are you going to stand here chewing off your lipstick?" Terrence remarked, while urbanely brushing snow from his broad shoulders. "We didn't have to come. It was your idea."

"I wanted to make sure," Mali said.

"That he was dead? He's dead. We read it in the papers, remember?"

Mali ignored him, and walked into the chamber. Sundry relations were gathered in groups around the morbidly decorated room, conversing about the more interesting living. Mali's sister Murgie bubbled away like a teapot in the midst of several greying great aunts. As she saw Mali, she gave a tiny, showy wave, and continued doing the social. Mali walked up to the flower bordered casket, where her ponderous old mother stood. Her mother was not in mourning—she wore a polyester pant suit of bright crimson. Mali touched her arm. The old woman turned from her detached evaluation of the corpse. Her bitter expression sagged into the kind of joyful anxiety that mothers wear for their unhappy daughters.

"Hello, dearie," said mother, kissing Mali tenderly. "I'm glad you're here."

Terrence, unnoticed, moved close enough to hear the whispered interchange.

"Why?" said Mali.

"Because, you know, it's hard not to feel pity for the bastard, when I see him like this." The mother waved in the body's general direction. "And your aunt is a wreck, and that's always a sorry thing, to see people grieve. I needed you here, Mali dear. I needed to feel hard about him again."

"Forgiveness does sneak up," Mali murmured. There was a moment of listening silence between the two women. "Did you know or did you guess?"

"I detected." Mother laughed sharply. The laugh sounded like the bark of a vigilant dog. "I knew it happened somewhere, sometime. It was only a matter of narrowing, narrowing, narrowing. You might want to tell somebody about it. I'd listen."

"I'd listen too," said Terrence suddenly, and Mali leaped again, as if touched by a dead hand. "I'd listen to anything you want to say, Mali. Hello, Other Mother. You look charming in red. Are you celebrating?"

"I'd have worn my dancing shoes if my conscience had let me," Mother said, while kissing Terrence on his closely shaved cheek. "So. When are you going to quit being the playboy of the Western world, and marry my daughter?"

"When she lets me. When she quits forgetting sometimes that I'm in the same room."

"Petulance, Terry my boy. Come along with your mother. We'll have a snort later on to celebrate together. A real likely way to commemorate the passing on of this sot, if I do say so myself."

"But Mali..." Terrence leaned protectively towards Mali, who was hovering in fascination and dismay over the wrinkled remains.

"C'mon," Mother urgently recommended. "It's going to take care of itself."

So Mali was alone with it, her uncle's body and her uncle's house. The shrivelled up yellow casing was covered up to the waist by the box. Its still abundant hair was neatly combed, and its face was posed in autocratic sorrow. It was a face that had been destroyed by alcohol and excess. Once it had been handsome and florid with youth and health and money. Mali remembered it in connection with the last house her uncle had owned, before he had let his vices eat away all of the family money. That house had been out of a gingerbread book, small, as neat as his wife and daughter could make it, filled with light, and plants, and the smells of good things cooking. It had a picket fence—houses in Mali's neighborhood didn't have fences at all, nor did they have flowers in the garden. What a glory it had been, that summer when she was five years old, to visit her uncle's house.

"But it didn't have enough beds" Mali explained to the corpse, as if a dead body could comprehend such an objection.

******

It was midnight, and the two girls were supposed to be sleeping. One of them, Dina, actually was, but Mali was having a harder time. Since Dina was athletic, and tended to sprawl over the bed, that night she had forcefully dispossessed her sister three times. Mali was tired of the night. It had been a day full of fun things, and it was a day that required child recuperation. Mali ached for sleep. She got up from where Dina had tossed her on the floor, and began to search around the house for sleep.

Mother and father couldn't be disturbed, Mali knew, and to wake grandmama would be unthinkable. Her cousin was sharing her bed with Auntie Melanie, and Mali realized instantly that there was no room for her there. Uncle Ted was snoring on the sofa, his body taking up the entire length. Cousin Fred was sleeping on two chairs in the living room. Murgie was in a dresser drawer at the foot of her parents' bed. Mali went around and around, from one room to another, trying to find a spot to lay herself down. It was then that the child heard a clinking sound in the bathroom.

Mali paddled to the bathroom door. Shyly, she pushed. It was uncle, his pajamas askew, drinking something yellow out of a bottle. Uncle was such a nice, refined gentleman—a teacher, a professional, not a working man like her father. Uncle stared as she peeped into the room, then began to laugh quietly.

"Mouthwash," he said. "Just mouthwash, ha ha."

She explained her problem to her uncle.

He knelt down in front of her, and breathed mouthwash smell in her face. He hugged her. Mali felt relieved.

"You just come in with Maud and me, little girl. Ha ha. With both of us."

It was only when uncle pulled her into the wide four-poster with her snoring aunt that Mali began to feel funny. He pulled her into his side, and held her close, and she felt something funny poking into her legs. When his hands started moving around, Mali tried to scream. But she couldn't because it was her uncle, and it was his house, and her mother and father would know and would not forgive her. Mali closed her eyes, and wished she could have a guardian angel to protect her like they said in bible class. After a long, long time, uncle fell asleep. Quietly, Mali got out of bed. She crept into the hall, crying softly, so as not to wake anyone.

In the morning, she was found by her early-rising father, sleeping under a rag rug in the hall by her parents room.

"I don't care what anyone says, he was a good husband to me," said a voice from behind Mali.

Mali turned, and looked into the vacuous face of her aunt. It was a face like plastic wrap, like pink cellophane. It had nothing behind it or inside it. It had been drained dry, by bill collectors, other women, and a life of moving from hovel to hovel. Aunt Maud had been dead for much longer than her husband.

"Was he a good husband?" Mali asked curiously. "In what way?"

It was painful, watching the eyes roll inwards, and to see the wife of thirty years seek, in vain, for something beautiful to remember, to wave as a flag. There must have been a time, but it had all trickled away, and sailed beyond recall. Aunt Maud's troubled frown was not for Mali, but for the treachery of memory.

"I don't remember, but it was so," came the conclusion.

"Do you miss him, Aunt?"

"Oh!"

The old woman held out her hands to the coffin, and there was longing in her voice. She began to weep. A stocky woman with straight hair gave Mali a push, and collected the relic.

"What has she been telling you?" Mali's cousin darted suspecting eyes at Mali. "You can't listen to what anyone says, it's all done with now."

"Never done," sobbed Aunt Maud. "Never."

A question formed on Mali's chewed lips, for her cousin, who was swollen up from inside from some constant hate. The Greek chorus of relatives said she was a lesbian these days. Mali tried to imagine what it would be like to be trapped for a childhood in the night at her uncle's house. It was the first time Mali remembered having such a thought. She looked around the room suddenly, wanting her own father.

"Angie, have you seen my dad?" she asked her cousin.

"He wouldn't come!" wailed Aunt Maud. "My own brother, and he wouldn't come. He forbade me to marry Ned, he always hated him. He wouldn't come, not even for me."

"Who wants him here anyway?" spat Angie. "Who needs more holier than thou? Men. They're all out of the same lousy pack."

"My father isn't," Mali found herself saying. "My father is an honorable man."

As if the negativism of the years had been shed like a moth molt, Mali knew the need to see her father, and apologise to him for—she didn't know what.

Mali liked to swing on the apartment playground, and would go there every day, and sit rocking for hours. She sang tuneless songs to herself, and decided what she would be when she grew up, besides rich and famous and pretty. Her sisters often speculated on who they would marry, and when, and how wonderful it would be. Mali wanted to be somebody, but she didn't want to marry ever. When asked by her skeptical sisters why not, her answer was: "Men are icky."

Dina was thirteen, and thinking seriously about such things. Murgie seemed born for tickling the beards of old men, and breaking the hearts of the boys. Mali sat on the swings, at eight years old, dreaming about airplanes, and sailing boats, and anything that would take her away. Uncle and aunt had come to dinner, and Mali had made good her escape. It was only in dreams that uncle's house went away, and Mali could pretend that she wasn't as bad as she knew, somehow, that she must be. Her mind was so absorbed in an attractive imaginary scene, that she didn't see or hear her uncle stagger out of the apartment back door. He saw her soaring up higher and higher, and came towards her.

"Ha ha. Hello little girl. Gotten pretty quiet lately, haven't you? Give uncle a kiss."

Mali leaped out of the swing, and ran to a safe distance. She stood twitching nervously with fear and defiance.

"I don't want to kiss you uncle, go away," she said.

"Is it a game, Mali? Do I have to catch you first, ha ha?"

"Leave me alone," the child wailed. "I'll tell Daddy!"

The uncle walked calmly towards the girl, something glowing on his intoxicated red face. His voice shrunk up to a whisper, he hunkered down and crept towards her.

"But you didn't tell daddy before, did you? I guess not, no sirree. You think I'm a bad man? I am. I'm no better than an animal. Are you afraid of me? Good. Be afraid, ha ha."

Mali broke and ran. She leaped onto the monkey bars, and pulled herself up. She sat there and whimpered, terrified. Uncle stepped beneath her, looked up at the seat of her pants. There was a blind sort of anger in his face. He grabbed for her feet, got hold of both, one on either side of the iron bars, and began to pull. He put his whole adult weight on her, and pulled hard, splitting her in pain. Still, she couldn't scream.

"Tell, and I'll make you pay. Tell, and they'll punish you, you little slut."

He let her feet go. They dangled above him. He began to saunter back to the house.

Mali, in a dim haze, saw her father emerge from the apartment. Her father had been a soldier once, and had a soldier's bearing. He marched up to her uncle, who replaced his evil face with an innocent smirk.

"I heard my daughter crying," said Mali's father tersely.

"I was just teasing her. She's too emotional. You pamper her, ha ha," said uncle man-to-man.

Mali's father looked at uncle, in the same way he looked at Mali when Mali tried to lie to him. It was like the plumbling of a lake. Father's eyes shot down into the depths of uncle like a harpoon. Then, with a soldier's display of military science, father dropped uncle with one strategic punch. Her uncle looked up at her father suspiciously.

"You ever touch one of my daughters, I'll kill you dead," said the soldier. "Just a friendly warning, Ned."

Mali fell down from her perch into her father's arms.

Mali began to search for Terrence, wanting him now as she couldn't recall wanting him. The best thing about her live-in lover, besides the fact that he could cook and wash clothes without going into hysterics, was that he maintained a respectful distance from her neuroses. He was sophisticated, could be a bit silly, was prone to hypochondria, and was vain about his looks. As an escort he was indispensible. As a lover, he was patient and uncritical. Theirs was a friendship that never got fearful or deep. Until lately. Terrence had been trying, in his own unaccustomed manner, to inject a more serious note into things. It was, for Mali, confusing.

He was at the door, flirting with Murgie.

"Why, you tawdry little minx, how dare you? Mali, darling, this sister of yours is acting like a person of no background. Do you know what she just asked me?"

"Oh, c'mon Terry, don't you Reaganize just a bitsy bit?"

Mali always admired the way Murgie looked. Dina was purely an earth shoe, an d wore natural beiges and comfortable baggies, but Murgie was a fashion plate. She always looked as if she'd been sprayed all over with some kind of laquer that kept everything exactly in place. It was a way that Mali tried to look, but couldn't.

"Of course I do. A tad of Grecian formula on the temples never hurt any man. Do you want your sister to be seen around town with an elderly gent? No not you! Now, about this uncle, Murgie. Quite an unsavory individual, I've been told. Many social misunderstandings, so to speak?"

"A letch and a sot," said Murgie, over Mali's protest. "For over thirty years. He tried to get into my pants when I was thirteen, you remember Mali, it was at Cousin Fred's wedding. I was going to tell Daddy, but didn't because I thought he'd blow an artery—his blood pressure, Terry, is not the best. Somehow the old man must have sniffed it out, though, because he and uncle started duking it out over the wedding cake. It was a scream! Don't you remember, Mali?"

"No," said Mali stiffly. "I don't remember."

In those days, it was mini-skirts, and Mali wore one such skimpy dress to the wedding, mainly because Dina and Murgie insisted. Mali was seventeen, having skin problems, and in her bookish stage. Some of cousin Fred's pals were going to be there, and both of her sisters were buzzing with speculation, would some of them be 'cute', would they ask Dina and Murgie to dance, and what did Mali think?

"If one of those jokers asks me to dance, I'll scream."

The reception was held in the party room of the Towers, and the liquor was running deep all night. Even Mali's father was a bit tight, and her mother was whooping it up with Aunt Maud in the corner. Mali hid from the pals, and danced so poorly with cousin Fred that he gave up and went to ask grandmama. After hiding behind potted palms and clumps of celebrating strangers, she decided to walk outside and cool her hot face.

It was snowy outdoors, and she stood looking at Hennepin Avenue. The fountain in the plaza was turned off for the season. Ice melted in her shoes, and she began to shiver. She turned to go back, and ran into her uncle's arms.

"Get away from me," she hissed. "Don't touch me, old man, or I'll knock you down!"

He *was* old. He'd shrivelled into a yellow stick, his golden pate was now silver grey, and he had veins making maps all over his nose.

"Always were a shy one, ha ha, but I knew what was under all that, ha. You've tried to get me going ever since you were a little girl, you whore. It was your fault, and now you want to make poor uncle Ned the heavy, ha ha. Well I got your number bitch, horny little bitch, ha!"

He reached forward, and pulled hard on the bodice of Mali's dress, and it tore, and she was frozen. Then Mali slapped her uncle hard, and he fell down in a snowbank. She stood above him, not believing that she'd done it.

"I've told them all about you, Fred, all his boys, everybody. You should hear what they're saying about you, ha ha."

There was blood on his teeth. As he sat in the snow, he wiped his mouth.

Mali ran inside. She flattened herself against the wall behind the palm, and died quietly. Then a defiant resolution ran into her from nowhere. If they all thought she was 'like that', then she would be 'like that', because it didn't make any difference what was true. Shaking, she walked up to the least attractive and nice of cousin Fred's pals.

"Hey, Jack. Want to dance, huh?"

Later, Mali's father knocked uncle Ned neatly into a bowl of potato salad. After the noise died down, the whole family left, and Mali gave Jack her telephone number.

At first Mali's parents thought it was a good thing, their wallflower daughter finally going out with men. It was only after cousin Fred called to warn them, and after Mali had moved out, and started to cover bad Jack with every bad jack in the deck that they had begun to understand that something was not quite right with Mali.

By the time Mali discovered how destructive it all was, she couldn't go back and change it. Nothing erased. Terrence was another in a long line of excuses.

Out at the cemetery, they buried him. Mali saw them gently lower the casket into the rectangle, and stood with Terry as they tossed mud and rocks on top of the box.

"He's really dead," said Mali.

"Yes, my dear. Dead and gone. Are you a better person because of it, or a worse one?"

Mali looked up at Terrence with a question forming. She could see that he was very angry, and Terrence avoided anger as an unappetizing emotion.

"My name is Terrence, and I'm a normal American male. I'm not symbolic of men as a species, and I do not pry. But couldn't you just for once see me, and couldn't I just *once* feel something that is not superficial, and couldn't I just *once* express it without your running for cover?"

"And if I tell you what happened, Terry? Will you leave me?"

"Tell me, and see."

She took his arm as they meandered through the headstones to the car.

"Then, I guess it began in my uncle's house..."

Casualties

RICK ALWAYS LIKED TO CALL HIMSELF a gay divorcee, and I suppose that's a pretty okay evaluation. He also called himself an actor, when he was in his cups, and I think that's even better. At the Watt House (the electric company, for the uninitiated) where we both worked the Saturday shift, nobody knew he was gay, nobody knew he'd been married, in fact nobody knew he was short until I pointed it out to a few people. He gave the impression of being tall. For a man five feet two inches high, that's acting.

How did we get to be the Saturday team? Well, I think it was because we both liked stories. People who do not want to be harrassed about their overdue bills usually come in Saturdays because they figure that the mean credit adjustors are home being mean to their kids and their dogs. So on Saturday, Rick and I got the deadbeats, and the stories! We heard bad kid stories, bad luck stories, old age stories, smashed car stories, unemployment stories, short-on-good-groceries stories, and more. Rick, who works credit, listened with complete fascination to all of them, then discounted the bills. I rang them up with a hip-hip and a good day sir or ma'am. It was a racket, I admit it, and we probably lost the Watt House thousands, but (as Rick would always add) we couldn't really be sure who was lying and who wasn't, so we had to give everybody the benefit of the doubt.

"Poor people shouldn't have to grovel," he would say, munching down the Chinese take out I picked up at the Nankin one hot Saturday in August. "I mean, think how un-artistic it is, grovelling poor people from coast to coast. Can I have some duck sauce?"

"Say, sportie," I responded, while handing him duck. "Lemme ask you a poisonal question. How gay *are* you exactly? That number that walked into your office this morning didn't look male."

"I never kiss and tell."

"Well, they all look like you import them from Aspen and Rio. What's wrong with all the overweights or understacks at the Watt

House?"

"How do I rate, you ask?" He grinned, and flexed his damn dimples. "I just convince all of them that I'm what they've been dreaming about. I mean, I find out their type and be it."

"Well, it doesn't work for me. To me, you look like you. Don't I have a type?"

"Nope. You have a father complex." His handsome miniature face got sober and shadowed for a second. "I ought to know."

It was a thing we became friends over, our fathers. We both had military fathers, and bitched about them constantly. Army brats know from fathers, let me tell you. We re-fight the Nazis on the front lines in our dreams. When other kids get electric trains, we get boxes of GI plastic soldiers, and our dads tell us about holding actions, and how to capture machine gun placements. There aren't that many machine gun placements in downtown Minneapolis.

Now it might surprise you to hear it, but Rick tried to join the army once, but he was too short, and they wouldn't take him. It didn't bend him out of shape too much, since he didn't realize at the time that we weren't fighting the Germans anymore. It was Germans that he wanted to battle. His dad was a war hero during World War II, and talked about it as if it were the only really important thing he'd ever done in his life, including fathering Rick. My father was a war hero, too, but in contrast, when he got out of the service he took all of his medals and his army uniform, wrapped them in a bundle, and threw them off a bridge into the Mississippi River. The only time my dad ever talked about Nazis was in his sleep, when he screamed about them. The rest of the time he didn't talk much at all. He still wanted me to know about the placement of heavy artillery, though. I guess, to him, it was still a useful skill for the average child to know.

So when the Nazis invaded downtown Minneapolis on a Saturday afternoon, let's face it, they didn't know they had a cashier clerk and a credit adjuster sitting right across the street with field marshall capabilities. If they had known, they would probably have stayed home.

That afternoon in August was hot like the tropics, but it was air conditioned in the Watt House, so we didn't care. We were playing around, acting out our lives for one another. Rick's favorite thing was to do snatches of plays, and to sing opera arias, and to talk about his lovers. I would make up long depressing tales about my messy childhood, my defunct medical career, and my lack of lovers. About that time, the glass doors in the front of the shop opened with a sucking sound. Heat poured in waves through the door, as two old people entered, one supporting the other.

We recognized them as regulars. Mrs. Kowalicek was a gnarled old woman, living marginally and with resignation on social security. Monsieur Alexandre Moreau was one of our favorites, a distinguished white-haired Frenchman famous for his excellent manners and partial payments. He mostly supported himself by tutoring French. Mrs. K. was sobbing hysterically, occasionally breaking into desolate wails. Alex was practically carrying her into the place, muttering comforting French phrases which I'm sure she couldn't understand.

Rick hurried to them, making physical contact with hugs and pats within a matter of seconds. I locked my cash drawer and went dashing out to join the trio, prepared with questions about purse snatchers and mouthy kids.

For a while, we had some trouble, as Mrs. K. kept wailing in Yiddish, and Alex rattled on in French. Eventually Alex took the lead in narrative, and we got the story.

"The war is never over," Alex trembled. "We come to Etats Unis, we think we are safe, but we are never safe anywhere. They are here, they are always here, even when we are old and tired."

"Who is here, Monsieur?" Rick pressed.

"The Nazis, the Germans. We see them marching, with clubs and armbands, our homeland."

"Out *there*?"

"Marching," he nodded, several times. "We see them on the street corner, passing out papers. No one stops them. No one arrests them with guns. Clubs in their belts. Armbands."

"Never, no more," Mrs. K. whimpered.

Alexandre straightened his thin shoulders.

"I was Resistance," he said proudly. "I fought them in the sewers. Many fought. Many died. Many did both, tous le deux." For a moment the language broke down, and long lines of French spilled out.

"Never, no more. No more."

"Brave lady was in war. In Nazi camp, was beaten and starved. She went up to Nazis. Tried to pull off the red arm band. They pushed her. They pushed her, and she fell. A long injury in the past, non?"

"That's awful!" I exclaimed inadequately.

"She cried that they are coming to take her again. They will not take her. I will stand. If the Americans cannot face these animals, I will stand."

He flung up his head like an old war horse, but he could hardly stand.

Our Saturday salesman, half asleep at the onset, was leaning out of the door. He nodded to us, whistled, and said: "Get a load of this!"

We went to look outside. Sure enough, the American Nazi Party was holding a demonstration on the corner of Nicollet and Seventh. I had a feeling of nauseated deja vu, like a person living through someone else's war might have. The khaki uniforms, the helmets, the glistening boots, the rigid military posturing, it was all there, like in the documentaries I used to see in grade school. One red armband lay winking on the ground in the hot sun. Good for you, old girl, I thought.

I turned to Rick. He was absolutely rigid. He commanded me (that's the exact word) to call the police. As I ran for the phone, I heard him say firmly to Alex: "Tell her they won't take her. Tell her that it's my homeland, too. Never, no more."

I got on the horn to the cops. I explained the situation to the laconic policeman on the end of the wire. He seemed amused.

"Lady, fringe elements are demonstrating all the time. So what's the big deal?"

"They pushed an old lady, and she fell," I insisted.

"Old ladies fall all the time..."

"She's a *Jew*! She was in a concentration camp! She's got numbers tattooed on her goddamn wrist, and you're telling me this isn't important to you? Where the holy hell were you raised?"

I was shouting into the phone. There was a thinking silence.

"Look, somebody is going to kick ass on these hoseheads. You want riot? You get riot, and it'll start with me!"

The cop turned terse and professional.

"Somebody will be out to pick them up in a couple of minutes."

After I slammed down the phone, I ran outside to join Rick. He was so small, I figured that he might need some help. I've never had much violence in me, but I had enough then to actually launch into any Nazi currently made in the U.S.A. Rick was there, but he had it all under control.

By this time, a circle had formed around the Nazi demonstrators. It was a circle of people my parents' age, along with some blacks, holding the papers that the demonstrators were passing out. The headline: Unemployment Rises as Niggers and Jews Steal White Jobs. It was a tense, unsure circle of faces, with an electric current of anger running from person to person. I closed with the circle. Rick was inside of it.

"Ladies and gentlemen! We now present Adolph and Friends Travelling Nazi Show. Bla-dah!"

He was declaiming in a loud hawkster's voice, as if he were selling patent medicines. Someone laughed.

"They sing, they dance, they goose step down the a-ve-nue. They swing their clubs, real imitations of the real thing!"

Everyone laughed. One of the red-faced Nazis pulled a club out of his belt in a menacing way. The circle closed in. He began to nervously swing it back and forth.

"Note the fine Aryan features! Thrill to the fakey phoney uniforms! Gasp as they show their muscle by pushing down old ladies, Jewish old ladies who summered in Treblinka! Oh, you kid."

He put one of his fingers under the chin of a nineteen year old blond boy, who pulled away, ashamed. The crowd began to get into the act.

"Hey, club face, your mother wears army boots! To bed!"

"My man!" yelled the black man with the panama hat. "I got your white job, and washing out toilets is a drag, you can have it back any ole time!"

"Hey, sucker, you wanna knock down my mother in law? Watch out she don't knock you down first! She's eighty six!"

"But children, children," Rick mocked. "Do you mean to say you don't like the boys? Dear, dear, dear. That's show biz. What shall we do with them?"

"Tar and feathers?"

"Crucify them!" shouted a woman.

"Nah! Circumcise 'em!" the black man commented gleefully.

The circle closed in, as howls of approval rent the air. The demonstrators huddled together, terrified, and that was how the police found them.

I don't know what would have happened if the cops hadn't arrived just then, but it would have been ugly. The Nazis were meekly escorted to the squad cars. The policemen tried to take Rick too, but the crowd protested so vociferously that they had to let him go. I backed away to let him take his bows. Watt House stock must have soared.

Stationed at the glass door were the salesman and Alex. Alex smiled weakly as I walked in.

"He made them a joke. This is true?"

"They are a joke, Monsieur."

"No," he said sadly, looking over at Mrs. K. "The war is never over all the same."

I was worried about her. She looked as though she might have a coronary. She was grey and passive looking. Over and over she kept saying a list of names. Everyone in the room had a casualty list, but hers was so long. Alex took her arm, and she began to shuffle out lifelessly.

Rick appeared out of crowd like a jack-in-the-box. He stood in the entrance, the sultry sun rippling behind him, the cool darkness within. He held a Nazi armband. He offered it to Mrs. K., who looked at it as if it were a dead rat.

"For you," he said. "A souvenir of a war we won."

It did make her better. She understood him, but refused to take it all the same. She kissed his cheek, patted it with a clawed hand, and left with the French Resistance fighter on her arm.

Rick was left with his armband.

"What the hell am I going to do with this," he grimaced.

"You're the fair-haired boy," I smiled. "You can either switch your political views, or have it stuffed and framed over the mantle."

He wasn't done feeling yet.

"You know, my father was in the group of soldiers who found the concentration camps at the end of it all."

"So was mine."

"Mine never got over it."

"Mine didn't either. He saw the devil then, and has been running ever since."

Rick nodded, and disappeared into his office. I went back to my cashiering cage to count money. As I was thumbing through some twenties, I heard him start humming. It was from a comedy movie, a little dittie called Springtime for Hitler. I chuckled softly and, assuming that the world was still safe for democracy, began balancing the take.

THE MINNESOTA VOICES PROJECT

1981

#1 Deborah Keenan, HOUSEHOLD WOUNDS (poems), $3.00

#2 John Minczeski, THE RECONSTRUCTION OF LIGHT (poems), $3.00

The First Annual Competition:

#3 John Solensten, THE HERON DANCER (stories), $5.00

#4 Madelon Sprengnether Gohlke, THE NORMAL HEART (poems), $3.00

#5 Ruth Roston, I LIVE IN THE WATCHMAKERS' TOWN (poems), $3.00

#6 Laurie Taylor, CHANGING THE PAST (poems), $3.00

1982

#7 Alvaro Cardona-Hine, WHEN I WAS A FATHER (a poetic memoir), $4.00

The Second Annual Competition:

#8 Richard Broderick, NIGHT SALE (stories), $5.00

#9 Katherine Carlson, CASUALTIES (stories), $5.00

#10 Sharon Chmielarz, DIFFERENT ARRANGEMENTS (poems), $3.00

#11 Yvette Nelson, WE'LL COME WHEN IT RAINS (poems), $3.00

Copies of any or all of these books may be purchased direct from the publisher, New Rivers Press, Inc., 1602 Selby Avenue, St. Paul, MN 55104 or from your local bookseller.